# The Japanese Box and Other Stories

JENNIFER ANNE GORDON

LAST WALTZ PUBLISHING

# Praise for The Japanese Box

The precision of observation here speaks not only to the honesty of the writer, but to the respect granted all phases of life; Jennifer Anne Gordon is on full display. Smart, full of character, vibrant. You will feel, you will feel big, and you will return, too, to the richest moments of your own history, landmarks that bring you to both smile and weep.

**–Josh Malerman New York Times best-selling author of Bird Box and Daphne**

I compulsively read anything Jennifer Anne Gordon writes. Like the best contemporary filmmakers stitching together grief and horror, her storytelling is a sharp needle that both pierces and tugs us close. Compulsive and genre-slashing, with exquisite, rhythmic prose, THE JAPANESE BOX is an extraordinary exploration of alone-ness that beats and breathes: *grief is horror, grief is love*. We as readers are drawn ever closer to this beautifully haunted narrator until we're face-down in the box with her. Does she feel us? She thinks she is alone. We all *think* we are alone. By the end we've become the ghosts in her black room, reaching out to gently touch her hair and whisper *we're here.*

**-Diane Zinna, author of The All-Night Sun**

### Praise for Pretty/Ugly

"Pretty/Ugly is a modern gothic filled with sensuality, dread and a dark kind of love that can only exist during an apocalypse..."

**-SA Cosby author of Razorblade Tears and Blacktop Wasteland**

"Pretty/Ugly, the story of two damaged people living in a dystopian nightmare, is an exquisitely written horror novel. But, is it really fiction? In these times, it seems chillingly possible... Pretty/Ugly is a deliciously frightening, absorbing tale that seems all too real."

**-Wendy Webb NYT Bestselling author of The Haunting of Brynn Wilder**

"More than a simply a fine horror fantasy, this is a highly polished psychodrama exploring early trauma, identity, life's exigencies, and fates – all woven together in a stunningly creative tapestry of a unique novel. Jennifer Anne Gordon is on the ascent as a literary figure of stature! "

**-Grady Harp, Top Shelf Magazine**

**Praise for Beautiful, Frightening, and Silent**

"This is a haunting exploration of loss and grief that kept me riveted from the first page to the last. The setting is exceptional, the imagery is vivid, and the writing itself is spellbinding."

**-Brian Bower author of Autumn Gothic**

**Dedicated to the Griefies**

*You are the ones that gave me the courage to open the Japanese Box and finally look inside.*

# Contents

# Simulacrum

It was never happiness I was looking for. All I wanted was the sensation of living in the moment, whatever it may be. I have spent years trying my hardest to live without memories; it seems impossible, but I am always trying to find a way.

Emme is standing in front of the mirror. I can smell her hair burning as she uses one electrical device to straighten it and then another to curl it. This takes hours, and it seems fucking pointless as Emme already has curly hair. I can hear her mumbling some bullshit she read online about Meghan Markle. The hair straightener and curling iron are teetering on the edge of the sink, which is filled with water, some ice cubes, and a bottle of Smirnoff Lemon Vodka that she has been sipping on all day like a baby with a bottle.

She slams the toilet seat down and kneels in front of it. She dumps some white powder on the seat and breaks it into a few lines, separating it with a makeup brush. I hate that I know it's an eyeliner brush. I hate that I spend time listening to her when she talks. Not just listening but hearing her.

I'm a great partner.

"Do you want any of this?" Her head pops up, and she wipes at her nose as she calls over her shoulder to me.

I sit motionless on the edge of the bed.

"It's just Adderall, so it's like coke, except it's good for you."

I don't say anything. I haven't said anything in hours, and I am not sure if she has noticed yet, and I'm not sure she ever will. She snorts another line off the toilet seat. She keeps talking.

"You know, if you don't pregame with me, you're just going to be a miserable shit at the party."

Partying is not the same as being asleep, but it's close, so I decide to get off the bed. My knee bangs into Emme's back, and she just keeps snorting those lines. I wash my face in the sink. The ice water burns my skin, and I wonder how much of the vodka she spilled in there. I lick my lips, and they taste like lemon.

In the mirror, I find my facial expression doesn't match up with the rage I feel inside. My eyes are blank and dead. I am an unblinking doll. "Fuck it, let's go." This comes out like a sigh, like a regret.

"Did you just say something?" she asks me, but she is already leaving the bathroom. She grabbed the vodka but left both the straightener and the curling iron plugged in. I reach up to do the right thing and unplug them but then think better of it.

Let it burn.

Let it all burn.

"We need to make a stop on the way. I need some groceries."

We walk three blocks through campus to the closest gas station. The fluorescent lights flicker, and everything has a swampy greenish hue that I can see from the street. When we enter, the air hums and strobes with the bad bulbs. Emme is wandering around. She has a twitchiness about her, like she is swatting away at invisible mosquitoes. I can only assume it's because she's been selling her Prozac to unsuspecting freshmen and telling them it's ecstasy. She doesn't need the money, but she does need the attention.

I stare at myself in the security mirror; this terrible lighting makes me look like a Victorian Death Photo. I smile, but it looks like a sneer. I don't recognize myself; even though I just looked at my own reflection before we left, I cannot be certain that I am the same person I was before. I cannot be certain if I am the same person now that I will be tomorrow.

"What the fuck are you waiting for? I'm ready."

I walk to the counter, and I finally notice what she has been scavenging the store for. The things that pass for her version of *groceries*. There are 3 boxes of gas store brand diet pills, a box of tampons, and several tabloids all featuring Meghan Markle and the shame of being a non-working royal. I don't know what that means, but I assume that Emme feels a kinship with her. In Emme's mind, she is practically royalty herself.

Her father owns a chain of used car lots. Emme has been in four of his commercials, and in the liberal arts wasteland that is our college, she is royalty. Emme's mysterious and complex to those who don't know her. Her hobbies include frantic masturbation followed by bouts of crying and selling prescription drugs and the occasional blowjobs to other members of freshmen royalty. She's an enigma, at least she thinks she is.

I am a lucky guy, in theory.

I gather from all the diet pills that at some point in the three blocks it took to get here, she's decided she's fat. The tampons mean she has her damn period, and I realize that this night won't get any better from here. I don't go down on her when she's bleeding. Fucking sue me. I'm a terrible feminist or whatever. I don't like blood. I don't like the mess.

She stares at me; her eyes are unfocused. Her expression dances between boredom and disgust.

"Well, aren't you going to pay for it?"

"Why the fuck am I paying for this? You're the one with the trust fund." My voice sounds scratchy and unused. I think of the kids in my dorm. The theatre majors who are constantly doing vocal warmups in the shower and in the halls. They sound like Rain Man. But maybe I should start doing this too. Use my voice, blow the proverbial dust off it more often, if you will.

*Unique New York. Three free throws. Red Leather, Yellow Leather. I thought a thought. But the thought I thought wasn't the thought I thought I thought.*

They sound like assholes. Never mind. I'd rather be silent.

"I thought we were on a date. You expect me to pay for things when we're on a date?"

In Emme's world, diet pills, Megan Markle, and tampons are considered a date, I guess.

"I'm the one on a scholarship—"

"I cannot believe you brought up your scholarship again. It's so embarrassing, not to mention selfish." She screeches these words at me, actually screeches them in a tone that I don't think is supposed to exist in nature. The sound of it makes me dizzy, and I try to brace myself on the counter. It's at this point that she reverts to her strongest and most powerful defense mechanism. She bursts into tears.

The gas station clerk looks at me like I did something wrong. I grab my wallet and pull out a credit card. I hate myself for giving in to her but then feel better when I see that the card I pulled out was Emme's.

I used it a couple days ago on Only Fans. Emme wanted us both to watch some Megan Markle look-a-like touch herself. It was all right, I guess.

We leave the gas station. Emme's still crying. She is noisemaking with angry, loud, guttural jags. I'm afraid that someone will stop us, assuming I've hit her or some shit. So I'm thinking about what to say, what perfect thing to console her before the cops or a good guy with a gun show up.

"So, you have your period. I guess that means we can't even fuck tonight, right?"

In theory, I guess this probably isn't the *right* thing to say, but before I can fake apologize, she grabs my arm and pulls me into the alley behind the gas station. I'm pressed into the small nook by the dumpster and a chain-link fence. I am trying to remember when my last tetanus shot was as rusty dumpster glitter falls onto my shirt. I try to get the words out, but before I know what's happening, my pants are down and she's on her knees. My cock is in her mouth before I am even hard.

I don't know which one of us I am more embarrassed for.

The alley smells like cat piss. The crying and sucking sounds make me think of washing uncooked chicken. I look down, and I realize that she's changed her hair color. I didn't notice before now, and this makes it easier to pretend she's someone else. I close my eyes and think of "Meghan Markle."

I explode in her mouth. I don't even bother to warn her that I'm about to cum. I know she hates not having warning. She probably doesn't want to waste the calories on me. She would rather binge on full-fat cheese than swallow little parts of me. Fuck that. I hate myself for the fact that even my orgasm has become passive aggressive.

She looks up at me, still on her knees in this alley; one of her knees is on top of an empty Cool Ranch Doritos bag. Gross. She has mascara running down her face.

"Do you ever wish I was someone else?" She sniffles, and for the first time, I see her for what she is. Who she is.

She's sad.

I know then that I'd rather hate someone than pity them. I don't respond to her question, so she just leaves me there in the alley with my pants still around my ankles. I bend over to pull them up, and I realize once the diet pills and tampons spill out that I am still holding the bag from the gas station.

Irony being what it is, in that moment, I don't wish she was someone else. I'm glad she's Emme. It makes what happens next have meaning. I come up behind her, and the bag is over her head before she even registers that I am there. She fights and gives off more energy than she ever has during sex.

The bag is a locker room.

The bag is a sauna.

The bag over her head is wet and angry but still clean. It's what I always thought sex would be.

It never was.

Now I am just a person, with a bag, in an alley.

It's then that I realize that killing someone may not be the same as love, but it's pretty close.

I smile.

And wonder if it counts if no one sees me.

My bitch mother went to a psychic when I was two. In the Reese Witherspoon produced version of my life, this would take place in a ramshackle shanty with peeling white paint. It would be next to a used car lot that doesn't require credit checks and where all the cars look like old police cars except they are spray painted white. The cars all look like soulless owls.

The psychic, "Madame Cilantro" (no joke), told my mother that I would see my life flash before my eyes and come to a reckoning before the age of 24.

My mother, in all her eloquence, said, "I hope it straightens him out. He's only two, but he seems like an asshole."

She told this story at all the holidays we celebrated, both before and after my dad left. I never laughed during her reminiscing. I'm not someone who laughs.

Yes, there are times I have made laughing sounds, but those always sounded and felt like a paint scraper being pushed up and down against an old wooden cabinet.

My laughter is green lead paint.

I stand in this alley now. I can taste that paint, and that imagined laughter is a noise that comes from my belly and then my throat. It comes out of my mouth, and I think, *This must be laughter*. It sounds like a siren, but it can't be that. No one knows what I have done. What I have become.

This sound—I think it's joy. It's laughter. It's becoming—

It's none of those things.

It's vomit.

It's messy.

I try my best to not puke—once I realize it's happening—all over Emme.

I know enough from watching marathons of *Forensic Files* while jerking off that it's best to not put too many fluids on, or in, the body.

I can hear the narrator now. Her mouth was bruised around the edges, her stomach only contained lemon vodka, semen, and then there would be a list of various prescription drugs. This list would end with Midol.

It's then that it really hits me—her throat, her stomach, it's filled with me, my cum. I lean down, slide her head out of the plastic bag. What happened in there is all over her head, her neck. It's all over my hands. I am splashed elbow deep in her homicide.

*Why am I getting hard again?*

I tilt her head to the side and see a thick white foam leak out of her mouth and onto the pavement. There are a few seconds of pride; I think about how good it felt when she sucked my dick, how much I came.

She has no gag reflex and no shame.

When I take the bag off her head, I smell it. It is her stomach acid, clouded over with a tinge of lemon. It's the fucking lemon vodka, and even in death, her shitty taste in alcohol ruins my night.

Why couldn't she have liked scotch? The only person I ever fucked who liked scotch was my dad's best friend. He was fifty-eight. His name was Greg.

I was fifteen, but that is a story best left in my repression closet.

I turn away from her and from the lemon smell of her death sickness. I'm proud of myself for turning her head so the liquid leaks out of her. I did not let her drown in herself.

In all of her shitty life choices.

In her sick.

I'm fucking tender.

I'm fucking kind.

I'm fucking hard.

Damnit.

It's then when it all washes over me. It's not my life flashing before my eyes, it's our life. Emme's life and mine. Our dates, all of which were more akin to the torture scenes in *A Clock Work Orange*, but instead of having to witness rapes and violence, I witnessed banality. Having someone throw their rapes at me, maybe that would have been better for me. Maybe it would have shocked me into being a good person.

It would have at the very least … been different.

I close my eyes and I see us.

Emme and me. Me and Emme. Our core memories.

Us.

We enter an art gallery. It's the kind of place with harsh fluorescent lights and large blank walls. "Industrial Space," a term that sounds fucking classy if you're in Chicago, but when you are a good 35 miles outside of Cleveland, you know it's just glorified climate controlled self-storage units—half of which have become martial arts studios, inexplicably all run by overweight, post midlife crisis Russians and Ukrainians. Emme's father owns this "gallery." It's his side project when he's not selling old police cars. He loves this building. He loves—his words, not mine—the *vibe*.

He's not Russian but finds the culture fascinating in its misogyny.

I look at the letters on the wall, the stenciled title of the exhibit.

*Ruined Childhood: The collected works of Handless Ben.*

Fuck this guy. Fuck his no hands. Fuck his art career. Most importantly, FUCK the fact that he wrote a bullshit blog that was picked up by the Huffington Post about how he has the right to call himself Handless Ben though he still prefers others to call him Handi-Capable Ben.

"These are amazing." Emme is almost breathless as she turns herself around and around. She is a dreidel in a black baby-doll dress and combat boots.

She stares at the art and feels its power. She looks closer to orgasm than she does even when I go down on her, and sometimes I do for what feels like hours. I've never seen this look on her face.

Bliss.

Fulfillment.

"You're fucking kidding me, right?" I barely finish talking before—

"You know I would never joke about art; art is sacred. It's not like joking about abortion, or the holocaust, or the moon landing."

I ignore the fact that she looks hurt or offended. I can't go there now. What I do say is, "Just because you pity-fucked a guy with no hands does not mean you have to think he's an artist."

"First of all, you fucking dick, it was not a pity fuck. We made love. WE MADE LOVE." She's shouting. Actual shouting.

Art buyers are looking, sneering, and judging.

"We were lovers. I'm sorry you have no self-esteem and you hate that about yourself. I hate it too, trust me.  I'm sorry he made me cum without hands, especially when I know fingering is your thing. It's less *messy*."

She rolls her eyes when she says messy.

I hate her right now.

"But I can see his work for what it is; it's dangerous, it's foreboding, it's about how no one is safe, that childhood is always on the edge of ruin ..."

"Jesus, first, don't say lovers, you're not in a Tennessee Williams play, and second, you did a ton of coke and then, like, a guy with no hands rubbed his stumps on you. You didn't do this out of love or out of anything ... you did this for the anecdote, the story you tell all your admirers, and you know it." I pause and look at the work hanging on the walls.

They are coloring book pages badly ripped from their books. I recognize Strawberry Shortcake, The Care Bears, one or two of the fake Disney Princess books—the kind you buy at a Dollar Store and are not technically Disney. I see all of these ripped out pages displayed in gilded, ornate frames.

I see cocks doodled in blue ballpoint pen all over these pages. I see low-rent Sleeping Beauty and Snow White with doodles of dicks drawn next to them. I look at the price tags of the "art." I see that if it's just a cock doodle next to a princess, it averages around $900; if that cock is shooting all over their un-crayoned faces, the price goes up to $1200; if there is hair on the balls, it's $1750. If it is not a princess and instead a puppy or bear ... it's $2000.

I hate art.

I see all the little red dots next to each sold piece of artwork. I turn to Emme, who appears to be enthralled by the elaborate picture frames, or maybe it's just all the red dots. Her pupils are dilated, and she is either high or in love. It's hard to say.

I see that she looks happy right now, and part of me wants that for her, but that part is silenced by my desire to make her just as miserable as I am right now, so I say, "Did you really like it when he put his dick in you?"

She looks at me. "Well, I never really like it when you put your dick in me. At least Handless-Ben is an artist ..."

She turns her face back towards the wall, towards the artwork. In this case, it's a grotesque geyser spouting cock next to Share Bear.

The way the fluorescent light of the gallery bounces off her face gives it an unnatural quality ... she is almost beautiful.

I have to stop myself from reaching out and running my finger down her jawline to her neck. I have to stop myself from falling into this trap of loving her or, worse, even liking her.

Fuck.

Fuck.

I could have loved her if she were not the worst person in the world.

When I open my eyes, I stand up and I am back in the piss-soaked alley. The bag I used around her head is in my hand. There is a dankness to it that feels heavy and comforting like a weighted blanket.

I put my fingers inside of the plastic. It feels like her pussy.

I miss her.

I killed her.

I miss her.

There is a sound that plaits itself like a braid …

Scream.

Vomit.

Cry.

I think I am making these sounds.

I am.

I am making them.

But I am not alone. I look down; I see the jaundice lemon foam come out of her as she laughs. The left side of her face still scrapes against the pavement. Like a scratch and sniff sticker, every time she moves, my world smells like cat piss.

Wet skin, wet uneven pavement.

Part of her rears up in a demented yoga pose. When she does this, half of her cheek peels off; it lingers in the alley like a burned egg … but still, all I smell is lemon vodka and piss.

I close my eyes, and I see the peeling paint of a "Madame Cilantro's" house. I want in my heart, or wherever my heart should be, to see my life flash before me like she said.

I want a reckoning. But all I hear is—

"You are such a pussy." She spits down the front of her dress; it smells like lemon. I think of summer. I think I would love her if I could, if I was capable.

I hear her puking and coughing. It smells worse than I thought it would have. It smells older. Like car lots and cancer. It smells like sitting on chairs and waiting for my turn—

I don't look at her.

I can't.

I do hear it, though ... a whisper between gags coming from her.

"I think this means we should get married ..."

I pretend she is still dead. That what she said was a ghost in a mirror. I pretend all I see are cocks doodled onto coloring books. I pretend I am still coming into her mouth.

I press the damp gas station bag into my mouth. It tastes like her. It tastes like me. I want to scream ... but before I do, I know I say ...

"Yes ..."

# The Japanese Box—Almost Thirteen

## (ALL THE TIMES I WAS NOT THERE)

There are two razor blades, fresh from the package, the Kmart blue light special.

I slipped them into my purse when my father was looking at cheap lingerie that he was going to buy for my mom for her birthday. Everything about that made me feel dirty; stealing the razorblades, the orangey red of the lace teddy my father thought would be *nice*.

There are 18 yellow Flintstone vitamins, 6 Midol, and 9 Tylenol. The Midol is there for the caffeine, maybe it would give me a heart attack, and the Tylenol because I heard it can damage your liver if you take them with alcohol. It seems like a shitty way to go, but it's better than nothing.

Going.

It's better than staying.

These things go into a wooden Japanese box. It is shiny but still somehow dusty. I never thought those things could work together, but here they are. They dance on the edge of yesterday, my yesterdays, and my father's. The box is meant for tomorrow and for all the tomorrows.

The razor blades are meant for me—

I could use them on a Friday night when my mom usually doesn't come home from wherever she has been until well past 2 a.m. She walks into the house hours after my father and I are asleep. She is a miscast villain. My sleepy Friday could turn into a Saturday morning, and no one would even wonder why I didn't wake up. They would think I was asleep, dreaming of being someone else.

The things in this box are bitter copper and sadness. I'm almost thirteen, and I am nothing more than bramble bush coated in bad skin and greasy hair. There is nothing left of me but hurt. It runs in this family. It runs in the dirty water that clangs in our pipes.

Every woman in my family has bipolar disorder or schizophrenia—I am just here waiting for my future.

Life: A short history of a decaying mind.

My mother sleeps in a cluttered room with an old record player filled with Streisand and The Carpenters. A room that we used to call *the porch*.

It's in the part of the house that is not heated, and when I have friends over, it's hard to explain. I shuffle my feet, and I don't say the words that my mother probably wishes she were dead, but she doesn't have a box filled with escape. Not like me. All she has is an unheated room and PTSD. She falls into her chair and leans back with her eyes closed. She's not drunk, but she was out half the night anyway.

Dad sleeps in their room in part of the house that has heat but not her. It's cold in its own way.

The cat who hid in the basement all night curls around her feet. My mother is exhausted in a way that I am years away from understanding. I hold a razor blade in my hand, and my mother is asleep; if she opened her eyes, I would make an excuse that "I just wanted you to show me how to shave my legs."

She is asleep. This razor blade can do anything.

# The Japanese Box—Not Quite Ten

Mom goes out on Friday nights. She speaks French with her friends and smokes long, fancy cigarettes. They're brown and smell like mint and fallen birch trees. She leaves the house with her blouse unbuttoned too far, but she hates it when I mention her cleavage.

"Enough. There's going to be a time when your little face and attitude won't be as cute anymore."

They aren't cute now; I know that. I don't feel cute. I feel itchy inside my throat from her perfume. Jovan Musk in an orange box. Everything in our life is from Kmart. Everything is the shade of red that only appeals to men.

I am two hours away from seeing the Japanese box for the first time, and two years away from the razor blades, and nine years away from realizing that my reflection is putting things into a box without my knowledge.

Right now, I'm just a kid.

Mom leaves just as Dad gets home from work. She smells like too much perfume. She is in the kind of pain that sounds like laughter and talking too much. Her eyes are sad, and no one in the house really talks to each other unless it's about food. Dinner? No Dinner. Just a block of sharp cheddar cheese and a knife that was born dull.

No one wants me to get hurt.

On Friday nights, my dad and I camp out on the pullout sofa bed. The brown tweediness is tossed aside, and the thin mattress over metal bars transforms our living room into a memory never captured in a photo. The sheets stay the same every week; it is like they live inside my couch. They smell like cats, plural, even though we only have one. The sheets are pale cream with roses. Some of the roses are faces, garish and obscene. They are comedy and tragedy masks. I told my pediatrician about the faces I saw in the flowers. He said it was a sign I was narcissistic or too neurotic for a child. I looked up those words in our two-volume navy blue dictionary that came with our Encyclopedia Britannica. I hated that doctor from then on. Later, when he was put on trial for molesting kids, I was happy. I wanted him to go to jail.

He didn't.

My parents still made me go to him once the families, the accusers, were paid off and the charges were dropped. I never forgot the comment, though, *narcissistic or neurotic.* He never saw the faces in those roses; if he had, maybe he would not have thought I was any of those things. Maybe I would have been labeled smart or sensitive. Maybe he would have known that the dirty blood that runs in my veins might be making me crazy like the rest of the women in my family. My mother would wear her blouses extra unbuttoned when we went to his office, but he never looked at her; he only ever looked at me.

Narcissistic. Neurotic.

So many screaming roses.

Those flowers take up most of the small living room. I lay on the edge of the sofa bed, and my face is a few feet from the television. There are reruns of *Knight Rider* on the TV. My Dad loves cars. I don't tell anyone that sometimes I go into the closet in the downstairs bedroom and kiss the back of my hand, *with tongue,* and I pretend it's David Hasselhoff. The hand never feels like what I think a kiss should feel like. It doesn't feel like the time the little girl my mom babysat played the husband during our game of *house.* It does not feel like when we both hid under the screaming rose sheets that time when her mom picked her up late.

This Friday night, the episode of *Knight Rider* has been on at least four times before this, and all I can think when

I stare at the screen is how boring cars are. How weird a leather jacket is; how cars that talk sound like doctors on other TV shows. How I've heard that voice before, but where?

Neurotic. Yes. Maybe my doctor was right.

My father is sitting back on the bed; there is a box of pizza between us, and he is drinking a Bud Light. It's not his first of the night, but I don't think he has gotten to four or five yet. "Did I ever tell you I climbed a volcano?" He purses his lips and blows into the beer bottle. It sounds like a train.

"You can't climb volcanos." I reached for the beer bottle so I can make it whistle too, but he doesn't see my hand. His eyes close before I get there.

"I did climb a volcano. And you know what else, you know Gramma's pearls? I got those for her in the ocean." He sips his beer. When his eyes open, they look like a long summer day. They are the color of the sky on afternoons when you start to miss going to school. He drinks. He doesn't do it to get drunk. He does it so he can fade away from the Knight Rider and the screaming roses. He does it to fade away from Mom in a low-cut blouse smoking a cigarette, speaking French.

Maybe he fades away so he can remember. A volcano.

I can't picture him at the ocean, finding pearls, climbing mountains. I have never seen his bare knees. I have heard from my mother that his legs are lumpy and pale, filled with shrapnel. I can only see him here, with grease stains on his knuckles. He fixes cars he can never afford. He brings them home on the weekend before their owners come to pick them up. It's Friday night, and they are in our driveway, but no one cares. Fancy cars that belong to someone else don't fool anyone; we are still the smallest house in the poorest neighborhood of this rich town.

My father's clothes smell like gasoline and oil. There will be a day when I smell a gas station and I burst into tears because I will miss him. But I am years away from that. Right now all I can think about is this supposed volcano. This impossibility of greatness hidden like seeds that never grew are inside this man. He sips his beer, and the pizza is cold, but he eats it anyway.

"There are no volcanoes here." Here in New England. Here in this living room. Here on this sofa bed. I'm skeptical. I hear my mother telling me that someday this thing I do, this always questioning thing, won't be cute. The air still smells like her perfume, and my throat itches and scratches at the memory. It seems so long ago, and it's only been three hours. I hate her for leaving me, even if it's just for a few hours. When she is here, my father's shoulders seem more relaxed and we are all able to breathe a little deeper.

I am barely breathing now.

"No, I was in Japan, back when I was in the *service*." He says *service*, and I understand what this means in a way that only a child could understand.

*Service* was why we can't watch reruns of *MASH* even though they are on right after the local news. *Service* was "war is not funny, little girl." *Service* was Korea. *Service* was eavesdropped stories about everyone thinking Dad was dead and "maybe it would be better if he were." *Service* was pearl jewelry he had made for his mother. *Service* was being missing for three years and coming home to a girlfriend that married someone else. *Service* were things that should never be said in a letter from his mom. *Service* was Christmas with food that he hated. *Service* was "it's better he learns this on his own." He bought the girlfriend a horse before he left for basic training; *Service* was that horse. *Service* was six months in a hospital that no one talks about. *Service* was him being paralyzed for months but there were no *physical reasons* for it. *Service* was exhaustion in the same way my mother was exhausted but still so much different. *Service* was not something he talked about, and I never asked—but I thought about it a lot. *Service* was me being quiet and chewing on the ends of my hair as he sipped his beer. *Service* was Mom leaving the house in a low-cut blouse. *Service* was my mother fighting a war we didn't even know about. *Service* was my father being petrified of wind. *Service* was this night, when memories tapped on the back of his teeth, begging to be let out.

I flip over on my back. I watch *Knight Rider* upside down, and it doesn't make it any better. I think about how kissing my hand didn't feel like anything. "Climbing a volcano doesn't sound like war." I can hear it. My mother was right; soon this wouldn't be cute.

"It's not always war. Sometimes it's ..." His words fade and then come back. "Sometimes it's the times between it all. Like dreams."

"Like wind?" Everything I say ends in a question mark, even when it's not a question.

I knew he would flinch when I said it. Maybe I did this to be mean, to push. Maybe it was to be the *me* that my mother said would not always be *cute*. I try to right myself around and plop onto my elbows in the opposite direction. My elbow is on the cold pizza. The half left over for Mom now has my elbow in it. I wonder if she will be able to taste my elbows later. I know I should not have said the part about the wind. I know I'm not cute, and I know there is pizza here that could taste like love, but I don't eat it. "What kind of dreams?"

"I have a Japanese box; I'll show it to you when you're older. And I have a fan from Mount Fuji. You can have that someday when I know you won't break it."

"I won't break anything if you show it to me now."

He finishes his second or third beer. He looks at but does not mention my elbow in the pizza. He flings the screaming roses to the side of the pull-out bed. His feet are heavy as they move into the kitchen, and then lighter as they approach the basement door, and then even lighter still when he stops on the creaky cellar stairs. They bow under his weight. His hands are rough and calloused; they are always stained with motor oil. When he moves the paper bags out of the crawlspace, it sounds like butterfly wings.

I hear the cat; she sleeps there with the secrets. She meowls in indignation.

He moves the metal lockbox that holds our family money. He doesn't trust banks or credit cards. He's never written a check. Behind the lockbox, there is something else. His hands touch it, and the house is filled with sad magic.

Dreams.

Wind.

I turn off *Knight Rider* before I am even asked. I hold my breath, and I catch my reflection in the television screen as it cools down. It turns dark green and then fades to black. There is a bright dot in the middle of the screen, and all I can think about is that my reflection looks nothing like me. She smiles, but when I reach up to touch my own face, I'm not smiling.

I don't know who she is.

# The Japanese Box–Close to Twenty

By the time I am on the Dean's List in college, there are six razor blades in the Japanese Box. There have been more and less over the years; sometimes it's an entire lady's pink razor with a flexi head. Perfect for bikini lines. I have never worn a bikini. Every part of my body is eating disorder fat, and every mirror is a funhouse mirror, except it's not fun.

When I look in any reflective surface, I imagine that it's not me; in fact, I know that sometimes it isn't me. I know that it's the twin that I should have had, the one that disappeared sometime between five and six months. That one lives inside me now. Chimera. Missing twin syndrome. It's amazing that this box, after so many years, can fit whatever

I need it to. It knows me more than I know myself. I find it full more often than not, though I have not willingly added anything to the box since I was fourteen.

I drink the vodka that my roommate keeps in the freezer. She is beautiful and slender, with wispy blond hair. She walks the way willow trees dance and bow in a summer storm. Our apartment is on the third floor; it's train car style. The summer is murder; everything is swollen with the humidity, and the floor groans like the Titanic about to break. I have a boyfriend, and we are in the dwindling, messy stage of break ups and boredom. We barely ever see each other, but somehow, I feel as if I would be worse off without him. Somehow, my existence would be less than it is now.

I spend the afternoon dunking popsicles in vodka. I sit in the window that faces out towards a video rental place that specializes in porn. When I look at the building, the back of my throat goes thick with embarrassment and shame. My roommate, Beth, is gone for a week, so I have plenty of time to find someone to buy a replacement bottle of vodka for her. I smoke her cigarettes and I eat her ice cream. I haven't had a real meal in days, and I am the kind of lonely that makes me feel buzzy and anxious all the time. I invite people over that I have not seen since high school almost two years ago. I kiss a boy who says he has loved me since the moment he met me. I don't believe him. I'm not lovable.

Weird Eric wrote short stories about me in high school and once gave me a present every day for a week: a bottle of orange Triaminic cough syrup, a box of Star Wars band-aids, a bouquet of tulips he had dyed blue. Then he asked me to prom. I said no. I didn't trust anyone that could want to love me like that.

He didn't really know me; just because we both loved *Twin Peaks* did not make us soulmates. But I kiss him anyway sometime close to midnight; the heat and the vodka have made things blurry. I haven't seen my reflection in days. I don't know where she has gone.

I don't miss her, but I am afraid.

The kiss is better than I thought it would be, but all I can do is hate myself for it. Maybe he was kissing the chimera; maybe she was kissing him. He apologizes and apologizes, a steady stream of "I'm sorry, I'm sorry, I'm sorry." He probably thinks he has taken advantage of me in my blurry state.

I leave him in my kitchen, and I go to my bedroom. He doesn't follow me, and I didn't ask him to. Sometimes a walk to a bedroom is just that, a walk. It's not an invitation. I find the Japanese box tucked behind a row of John Irving books on my shelf. *The Hotel New Hampshire* is water damaged and smells like a clogged sink. The razor blades have gone from six at last count to eight. Three of them have rusty edges, and one is completely blanketed in rust. I nudge that one with the edge of my pinky finger, and parts of it crumble. It leaves a mark on the bottom of the box like a photo being removed from a wall. With the razorblades, there is a torn page from the journal I kept when I was sixteen. When I look at it, I don't know why it's there. It was just from a normal day. A day I don't even remember, actually.

Why did *she* put it here? The box starts to smell like the ocean and Grandma Rita's pearl ring.

I reach for the shiniest of razor blades and make a delicate cut on the inside of my left wrist. It's shallow. "Across the street" is how to do it if it's a cry for help or a desperate plea for attention. "Down the road" is how to cut if you mean business, if it's the end to the story. I just went across the street. I look out the window of my room and can just make out the men coming and going from the porn store.

Across the street.

My blood is thin from all the vodka, and a brilliant red streamer dances down from my wrist like a barber shop pole. I move my arm in a weird way; my elbow seems to bend backwards as I try not to get blood on the carpet. Beth will kill me if we lose the security deposit. When she gets angry, her skin swells with red hives that start at her mouth and trail down her chin and neck. I walk in a zigzag; I don't think I'm that drunk, but everything feels like a dream. The heat. The popsicles. The kiss. I leave *The Hotel New Hampshire* on the floor. I find Weird Eric in the kitchen; he is holding his head in his hands. There is a green popsicle in a coffee cup in front of him. The room smells like limes and car exhaust.

Someone says, "I think I need a band-aid." I think it's me, but I am not sure if I opened my mouth. I let the blood drip on the linoleum … and maybe I am bleeding more than I thought I was.

"Oh my God." Weird Eric grabs my arm and squeezes like a tourniquet. I feel him tugging me towards the bathroom. It must feel like he is dragging rocks. Heavy. Awkward. I try to linger by the window. I'm distracted by all the comings and goings of Mike's Porn Video Palace.

"That guy looks like my dad." *Did I say this out loud?* I thought somehow my face was bleeding, but it's not. I'm crying, and I feel like I might throw up, but I have trained myself to not do that—not until I want to. There isn't much inside me. Just popsicles and vodka, and maybe my absorbed twin.

She would have changed our family into something less ephemeral. Instead of chalk on a sidewalk praying it wouldn't rain, we could have been an oil painting. We could have been permanent. A family portrait.

Eric shakes my hand over the sink like I am a dog holding on to an open pair of scissors. The rusty razorblade bounces off the porcelain and shatters into two pieces; one of them is already turning to dust as I look at it. It has already turned into yesterday. I never knew rust was so fragile.

"Shit, when is the last time you got a tetanus shot?"

"But—I didn't use that one. The rusty one is still in the box …"

He doesn't listen. He just turns on the hot tap until the water that comes out of the pipe is almost white. He holds my arm under the stream until my pale skin is a pink, puffy jacket, and the thin slice on my arm is barely more than a papercut. He grabs a towel that is already stained, bruised with reds and purples from my Manic Panic hair dye moods. When he presses it into my arm, it hurts more than the blade did.

"Careful, that hurts," I whisper.

I don't want to disturb the feeling in the room, the feeling that maybe he would kiss me again. The feeling that he would say sorry again. The feeling that I should have gone to prom with him.

The feeling of falling down a flight of stairs.

He doesn't kiss me.

He drops the towel on the floor. "You really scared me," he mumbles as his eyes search the sink. The rusted blade is gone, and right now neither of us know if it was ever really there.

"I scared myself." I smile at him, but he doesn't smile back.

He opens the medicine cabinet and sees the boxes of caffeine pills and tampons. The only other thing in there is a box of Star Wars band-aids and a dusty bottle of orange

Triaminic. He doesn't mention them; he just puts a few Han Solo bandages on my wrist.

When he closes the medicine cabinet, I catch a glimpse of myself in the mirror. The *me* that lives in the mirror has already left the room. I see her shadow in the kitchen, a freeze pop in hand.

All of *my* reflections are empty. I am three years away from seeing myself again.

# The Japanese Box–Not Quite Ten Part 2

I didn't expect a cardboard box that smelled like the creepy door to the root cellar, but here it is, plopped between us on the screaming rose sheets. There are little pieces of it falling from the corners like dirty snow. My eyes itch, and it is hard to breathe being so close to it.

I am a month away from my first asthma attack.

My dad brought another beer in with him. He pulls it out of the corner of the box like a magic trick. He drinks at least half of it in one long, slow sip. This time, he hands the bottle to me, and I blow into the top of it. It toots like a train.

Small talents.

He smiles, and his eyes crinkle in the corners. They went from cloudy to clear skies with just a cloud burst of happiness. It is the weather of his moods. These are the moments between the wind.

His biggest fear: it is the weather of our life in this house. The moment is there, and then it's gone. It is ephemeral, like a family with only three people.

I look at the TV screen, and the little glowing dot in the middle is gone now too. The girl who is pretending to be my reflection looks like me again, except sadder, smaller, and maybe a little meaner. The television makes a low-pitched hum, and then it goes silent.

My reflection is prettier than I am; my reflection is still cute no matter how she behaves. My reflection doesn't chew on the ends of her hair when she is nervous. My reflection is never nervous.

There are parts of me I have to inventory, things I need to do to prove I am real. I scratch at my eczema until I see bits of blood and skin under my fingernails. I smell my hair—*my hair* always smells like coffee. I reach up and trace the bump on my nose. I don't need to look at my reflection in the TV. I know it's there. I don't know if *she* has a bump on her nose or not. She probably doesn't.

My beautiful vanishing twin.

*I* broke my nose when I was seven. *I* slipped on ice and never caught myself; I just fell into an explosion of red that tasted like pennies. School pictures were that day. My eyes were puffy, but they were one day away from darkening into a purple bruised sky.

My reflection doesn't get school photos. She died in my mother's stomach, next to me. Eventually, she disappeared.

She is nothing I should think about, except I do. When I look at the TV again, she's not there. No one is.

*Service* is looking for your reflection and realizing you don't have one. My father is not in front of the television. I don't know if he has a reflection.

My fingers pick at the cardboard box like it's a scab. "This box doesn't look Japanese." I wait for a smart-ass reply from him, but instead, he leans back on the sofa bed and waits for me to say something. I look at the reflection in the TV. I can see the screaming roses, but that's it. Just an empty sofa bed.

I close the pizza box and put in on the floor, tucking it under the couch for safe keeping. I hate my mother for not being here and for not eating her half of the pizza with us. Everything in the room feels like walking over unsteady rocks.

I didn't know that a cardboard box could be so terrifying.

In the box, there are letters written to his mother that he sent from basic training. His handwriting is a rough combination of half cursive and half print. Underneath all the words about what he was eating in lieu of a family Christmas dinner is a sense of loneliness that makes the blood rush in my ears. A windstorm over the ocean.

It's always there. Wind.

I don't know why he has his letters to her but not her letters to him. Why is this all there is? The frayed brown string they were bundled together with falls to the floor. Our cat's paw reaches out from under the couch, and like that, the string is gone.

"Go on, just be careful with what's in there." He tilts his head away as if what I am doing is causing him pain.

"Did you like being in the Army?"

"It was the Marines."

He doesn't answer my question. My invisible reflection screams in my ears. She sounds like a storm. I take out a hand-painted narrow box that hold chopsticks; they are still bound together.

"Did you like being in the Marines?" Before he answers, I separate the chopsticks with a loud snap. My father flinches like he was just slapped.

"Yeah. I liked it." His voice is all one flat tone. He is lying. He's not a liar, but he just lied. I understand that protection and lying are both different sides to the same blanket on this fold-out bed; one side is scratchy, the other is fuzzy and warm. One side of the blanket is home, and the other side is whatever *service* was.

I put one of the chopsticks above my top lip and scrunch my mouth up towards my nose. The chopstick wobbles like a wooden mustache. I hand the other one to him; I have to poke him in the hand a couple times to get his attention.  He copies me as if we are un-vanished twins. I look at the reflection in the TV again, wondering if we are there. I wonder what she is doing. If she has come back. When I see her see me, she looks angry. Jealous. When my reflection grows up, she will wear my mother's perfume and I will hate her too.

My mouth goes slack, and the chopstick falls to the side of the sofa bed and then rolls onto the floor. The cat paw is out again, and with that, the chopstick is gone. We can hear it pattering against the pizza box like a drumroll.

"I told you to be careful." He is sitting up now. This time, I flinch, even though he has never hit me. His wooden mustache is now on the coffee table. His beer bottle sweats and has made a little pool on the only nice wooden table we have. We are not the type of family to own coasters.

He slides over to me and takes the box away as I lift an envelope of black and white photos from the bottom of the box. A stack of photos of my father. He is thinner and leaner than I can imagine him being. His arms are wrapped around the shoulders of two friends. They look like they are at the top of the world. There is a crater behind them. Their smiles are wide, but their eyes are tired. The next photo is almost the same shot, except none of them are looking directly at the camera and all their shoulders are slouched a little.

"Are these your friends?"

"Yeah."

"Are you still friends?"

I have never seen my father with a friend, never heard him talk to one. There are guys at the garage, but are they friends? I've already flipped to the next photo: my father planting an American Flag in the top of the mountain, near the mouth of a volcano.

"They're dead."

No one has said that word to me in years, not since our last cat; Thimble's liver swelled up, and he was taken away in the night. I drop the photos and make sure to nudge them back onto the couch before they fall onto the floor and fall victim to the cat's needy and bored orange paws.

"I want to see the fan you told me about."

"It's in here somewhere." He digs around in the cardboard box. The room is musty, and my eyes are starting to feel prickly around the edges. There are stacks of papers he takes out of the box and just sets off to the side. One more photo falls out; when I pick it up, I see it's my father. His body is bandaged, and he is in a hospital bed; he is maybe 80lbs at best. I have no idea that photo is also a crystal ball.

It's the future and it's the past. I am fourteen years away from knowing that.

He hands me a Japanese box; it is black wood and hand painted with cherry blossoms and my father's volcano in the background. When I open it, it smells like the root cellar. The air is stuffy and filled with secrets. There are two little boxes in there, and a little cardboard folder that is well-worn on the edges. The velvet boxes hold more promise at first sight; they are much more alluring than dusty cardboard. The boxes remind me of the ones my birthday necklaces come in. The gifts are all always hideous gold color and peridot. My neck turns green after wearing them. My first thought when I balance these boxes in my hands is *Jewelry*.

I'm excited until I open the first one, all I see is a silver star pinned to what looks to be a red, white, and blue spelling bee ribbon. The other one is a purple heart dangling on the edge of a pretty ribbon. "Can I wear these?"

"No."

"Do you wear them?"

"I did when I got them, but that's it." He already has the boxes in his hands, and he is closing them back up. *Nothing to see here.* He reaches into the cardboard and pulls out something else. It's small and wrapped in a worm-eaten silk scarf that is painted with orchids. "Here you go; I found it."

I'm not even listening. My reflection is screaming again in my head. She howls like the wind. My eardrums pulse in and out with it, they hurt, and I am afraid that soon

I won't be able to hear anything at all. I'm on the top of a mountain, standing next to a volcano. I have the little cardboard folder in my hands, and I am looking at the photo inside.

A woman, obviously beautiful in a way my mother isn't. She is beautiful in a way that I am not. I am not made from his past; I am not made from the man who climbed volcanos. There is a certain tone to a black and white photo that even without color, I can tell she is wearing red. There is a shine to it, a depth, an *otherness*. A red slip.

I remember the Kmart red lingerie.

This is not that.

The woman in the photo has an *otherness* to her. She is not the woman I heard my grandmother whisper to my mother about while they spent the afternoon playing gin and drinking scotch. This is not the one from *"back home,"* the one who thought my father was dead, the one who married someone else. The one who got a horse before my father went away. This is a woman with jet black hair; her skin is not white in this black and white photo. I realize when I try to lift her up and out of the dusty worn folder where she lives in my father's memories, there is more than just this one photo. They fold out like an accordion.

Each image is the same but different. She laughs, she smiles, she looks serious and stares into the camera, her slip dangles down her shoulder. She's happy, she's sad. She's alive, she's a ghost. She is a memory, and she is in this room with us now.

She is here, and I don't even have reflection.

The last photo in the accordion is her and my father. An old photo trimmed to fit in this little folio. His face is mostly cut off. His skin is so pale next to hers. She is beautiful in the same way that the dolls at the Chinese food restaurant are. The ones I always beg for at the cash register. The dolls I reach for as my father says he'll *go wait in the car.*

I can understand now that this is one of the places my father goes to when his eyes get sad and far away. Weather coming in over a mountain.

Wind.

Clouds.

Volcano.

He is somewhere with her, or bandaged up, or on the top of a mountain with an American flag; he is somewhere that is beautiful, but it howls ...

All of this happens as my father unrolls the silk scarf and it turns back to silkworms in his hands. Dust and memories. I am reading words on the back of a photo that say, *"Johnny, I will love you forever. Don't forget us."* I think the woman must be talking about herself and her reflection.

My father has the fan from Mount Fuji in his hand. He waves it back and forth, and the stale air of all his yesterdays blows against my skin like a summer-sweet kiss from afar. Underneath the last photo is a little black and white of a baby. Small hands in little fists by its face. My father's nose, unmistakable on the not white skin of this black and white photo.

"Who is this?"

The photos are snatched out of my hands before I understand what's happening. The fan from Mount Fuji is still open next to him. It's ugly; it's not what I thought it would be when we opened this box. When I turn to the TV screen to see myself, I see that there is nothing there. Just a reflection of my father. I've gone missing again, and I don't know when I will be back. The wind kicks up inside my head. It screams; it howls. The weather inside our house changes.

So do I.

# The Japanese Box–Almost 24–Where is the Japanese Box When You Need it?

There is a fuzzy time between bravery and stupidity that I live in. I have no money, but I work hard. It's all retail and clothes hangers and men's high-priced shirts. Sometimes customers from earlier in my shift call the department store and ask for me. I hear them masturbate on the phone; sometimes I listen; sometimes I leave the phone hanging from the receiver between Men's Big and Tall and the public bathroom at the back of the store.

I know which mirrors in the store are fat mirrors, which ones are thin mirrors, but I can never tell which ones I won't have a reflection in. Those are always changing.

My apartment sucks, and so does my job—but it's a life. I am coming up on the bad side of my early twenties. The making decisions time. The making choices time. I change my major over and over—I lose money every time. Psychology. Communications. Photography. English. Art History. Theatre.

My father told me that *"Theatre majors just become secretaries."* He half whispered, half wheezed this from his bed. He's sick. We don't talk about it, but we let his impending farewell press against our skin. He smells smoky and sour. I tried to remind him of the time that he gave me the fan with Mount Fuji on it. I tried to remind him of the Japanese box, but he told me that it never happened. He looks at me like he doesn't recognize me.

That night when I got back to my apartment, I looked in the box, and all that was there was a black and white photo of a woman in a slip. The bottom of the box had little rusted-out ghosts from the razor blades. They are gone for now, but I don't know when they will be back.

Weird Eric has long since stopped returning my calls. I wore the Star Wars band-aids on my wrist even after the shallow cut healed. The band-aids smelled like my bathroom and felt like choices I should have made differently. When my friends started to change their names to Zoe and Xantha, I should have done something, but instead I am here, just Jessica, packing for a spring break I don't want to go on.

I hate the sun.

Florida gives me hives.

I feel my mother, my grandmother, and all the women in my family's mental illnesses wafting in from Miami Beach. They smell like low tide and hot garbage. I feel the trauma from the abused women of my family reach up from the shallow seabed and grab my ankles.

I remember my grandmother Eileen the one time I met her; *"Only whores paint their fingernails."* I can still feel her fingers pinch mine.

My fingernails hurt, and I looked for a reflective surface, I looked for any other version of me, but there were none. I only saw my fingernails, and even at the age of eight, all I could wonder was who painted my nails that way?

Not me? Certainly not me.

They were salmon pink, the same color as the finest houses in "Little Havana" where my grandmother lived. Lizards skittered across her front yard. Everything was dried weeds and bleached rocks. The lizards climb trees and then they were invisible. The bark writhed and squirmed in the sun. It never stopped.

On that trip, I slept in a room with a picture of Jesus on the wall.

He was beautiful and gory—some weird bloody and handsome white fantasy. His eyes followed me while mother and grandmother fought like cats in the next room. They smelled like juniper, beer, and suntan lotion.

It was August. I was eight. My grandmother put mittens on my hands to hide my pink fingernails. She put mittens on my hands so I wouldn't touch myself with my whore-hands in the night while I was supposed to be sleeping

My palms were sweaty all night, and I could not sleep with Jesus watching. I tried to find myself in the reflection of her television; I was there and then I wasn't. The me in the TV wasn't wearing her mittens. The me in the TV was proud of her baby whore fingers.

The real me was happy to have the mittens on, even if I was uncomfortable.

Part of me is still there in that room with Jesus watching. I am there with the daughter of my mother's best friend. Our arms and legs are sunburned. Our skin peels, and underneath are layers and layers of *why we are here?* Layers and layers of *why didn't your father come with you?*

Baby whores.

I hate Florida. My feelings never changed.

But—it's spring break. I am traveling there with a girl who I might be in love with, but I don't have the words to say it. What I want to say is that when I look at her, I feel like a building has collapsed down onto me. I want to tell her that she makes me feel lost and crushed. I want her to know I mean that in a good way. But—I don't have the words.

I have not fucked my boyfriend for seven months, and even I know that at this point, *boyfriend* is a sad term. *Boyfriend* is a half-written fiction I don't know the end to.

Florida and Siesta Key are sunny orange. The air will taste like juice and empty calories. We are going to visit my friend who walked six miles every day to my house when I was seventeen going on sadness. My mother paid him to paint her bedroom turquoise, then a different shade, greener, then added blue ... every day. Her room was always changing, just a little. I called it madness green.

He was the only one who understood what I meant when I said it. When he was done painting, we would play with a Ouija board, we would walk in cemeteries ...

I thought I loved him but never told him. He had to have known, right?

That was way back when I was seventeen, and then eighteen. That was when I hadn't seen my reflection in almost two years. I didn't know where she was, but occasionally, I saw her scars.

Then I got a boyfriend. The *friend* moved to Florida. I am years away from him leaving for Europe a week after I tell him I am getting married.

After he left, that first time, we exchanged letters. There was no romance, but there was an understanding in the misunderstood. We missed each other in the way that best friends do.

More important—we missed each other in the way that people who have seen the same ghosts and believed in the same demons do.

He knew about my *reflection*, my twin. He saw her once. He believed in her. He knew her face, the way it was different than mine. He had a look in his eyes when he talked about her. He was afraid of her and maybe more than a little in love with her.

I didn't want to ask what happened when he saw her. What they may have done. I remember he told me that sometimes ghosts weren't dead at all. Then he wrapped one of my curls around his finger, again and again. He looked out the window, his eyes haunted the way my father's eyes were.

It was the wind.

Yes.

It got to him too.

I am packing now for this trip, and I don't know what goes in the suitcase. How do I pack to spend the week with the girl I might love to visit the boy who left me?

How many bathing suits do I bring?

How many dresses?

Do I bring cute underwear?

I think about the Japanese box, and I know I can't leave it here in this apartment unattended. These days, the box is tucked behind vampires and magical realism. It's hidden behind Anne Rice and Gabriel Garcia Marquez novels. I think there is no harm in tucking the box in the bottom of my bag. When I lift it, it feels light, and when I shake it, it sounds like it's filled with dried leaves and moth wings. It sounds like secrets. It sounds like whispers while hiding under a pullout couch. It sounds like—

I decide for the trip to tape it closed, and I don't care about peeling the paint from it. There is nothing dangerous in this box—not now.

I know it's just old letters.

They're from *the friend* in Florida. But these are not friendship, they are more than that. These are two people remembering something that I do not. These are two people that shared something that I was not a part of. They are one half of a conversation that I was not there for.

Who has he been writing to?

They are addressed to me and responding to me. But I am not who he has had this three-year conversation with.

Some of the letters are flirty and benign, so many lines of "if only we had …" Other letters are dark and strange, as if he is writing to someone in a hospital or prison. One isn't a letter at all, just an envelope of sea glass and small shells with perfect pineal rings.

I put the taped-up box with the letters on the bottom of my travel bag. On top, I have two one-piece bathing suits.

Black.

Royal Blue.

They are sexless and give big ashamed-of-my-body Victorian vibes. My belly has never seen the sun. This is not the time to take that emotional risk.

My room already smells like baby oil and sunburns, and I haven't even gotten on the plane yet.

When I look down at my hands, I see that my square-bitten fingernails have been painted salmon pink without my knowledge. I pinch my fingers to make sure they are real; I feel the ocean rush in.

My walls no longer have vintage Marilyn Monroe posters and collages of Depeche Mode and The Cure. Those are all gone.

Now, they are replaced with skittering lizards on every surface. They turn my walls into trees, and everything is too alive. When I close my eyes, I feel the judgmental eyes of the beautiful but not realistic hot-white-Jesus staring at me. My head hits the pillow and then I am—

# The Japanese Box—After Florida

I wake from dreamless sleep. My room is hot and muggy as if I had been sleeping under too many blankets, but my bed is bare. My mouth is dry and familiar. When I breathe, the insides of my cheeks feel like they are sliced in thin little lines.

Tally marks, or paper cuts. When I open my mouth and cough, I pull out fragments of letters; some are gummy and wet like papier-mâché, others are still dry like ripped up pieces of a ransom note.

I see his words but can only imagine hers.

My pillow crinkles. Stuffed with paper—even more letters. My body is sticky with half a story.

A love affair I never had.

My bag is open. The bathing suits and assorted *cute shorts* are strewn on the floor.

Unpacked.

Things are tossed like a breadcrumb trail, and my apartment looks like a bad episode of *Law and Order*. My boring underwear are nowhere to be seen. The three pairs of Victoria's Secret underwear that I had decided not to bring are there, though.

Dirty.

There are two sad swimsuits and a dress that I think makes me look pretty, but really, it's a vibe more like Anne of Green Gables before she got hot.

*All* of it smells like salt water.

I reach for the bathing suits; they are damp, and there is fine white beach sand in the crotch of both suits. A pair of the cute shorts is packed with sand-covered flip-flops in each pocket. There is a fully used Kodak instant camera tucked into a box of tampons.

When I get to the Japanese box, I see that it's empty. Traces of fine sand are hiding like spies in the corners. Carved into the bottom of the box are the words "Missed you. Wished you were here."

I pick up the phone in my room, dial zero for the operator. Ask her the time, ask her the date.

I've been home from Florida for two days.

I bumble from reflective surface to reflective surface. Windows, my shiny dance trophies, my roommate's old-school jewelry box with a spinning ballerina, and the microwave. I finally see myself again in the ill-fated medicine cabinet.

It's me. I'm here. My mouth is lipstick bruised from kisses I don't remember but would not have turned away. There are bite marks on the back of my neck and yellow green fingerprint remnants against my ribs and bare belly. I check further down; my fingers press against me but don't go into me. I am not sore.

I'm fine. It's all fine. She took my spring break from me, but she didn't do anything I would not have.

I wonder whose fingers match these prints. The girl I might love or the friend who left ...

Does it matter if next time I look at my body, those fingerprints are dream-fiction?

Or memory.

The *friend* who left calls six times over the next two days. I never pick up the phone.

*She* never calls. When I go back to work on Monday, I am sunburned and lonely. *She* is gone, gave her notice when we came back and never showed up for her next shift.

I am almost twenty-five, but I am going on invisible.

# The Japanese Box—Almost 40

I've given up on the time I've lost.

I open and close the Japanese box.

Again, again, again, again, and again—like Pac-Man.

It's empty.

It's full.

It's a baby photo.

It's me.

The carved missive from years ago is still there, but it sleeps, and I find it again like a grave rubbing.

Her words. My words.

*Having fun. Wish you were you were here!*

Everyone I loved back then is gone. I whisper my hopes into the box.

Nothing.

I whisper my fears into the box.

Nothing.

It has been years since the box has changed, and every time I look into a reflective surface, it's just me.

*Maybe I was born this way ... maybe it's better living through medication.*

I turn away. I come back. I try to catch her, but all I hear is wind. All I think about is *service*.

All I see is me. It's not enough.

I miss her. The reflection I never saw.

I am lonely for someone who was never real.

# The Japanese Box–Almost 42

I try to find her in my father's wind or in the band-aids from Weird Eric.

One Xanax and one Ambien.

No.

She isn't there.

I mix it up, half and half, sleep deprivation and sadness. I look for her.  I catch her out of the corner of my eye. She is in the shiny part of a dirty pan.  And then she is nothing.

I look for her in vegetable oil and stainless steel.

She is there, but she doesn't stay. She blurs and then slides away like paint on a canvas.

Art. But. Not.

She just waits on the edge of my life. She is part of me.

Chimera.

She is my Japanese box.

I miss her. I miss her more than the life I could have led. I think of her more than the choices I could have, should have made.

I am nothing, just a part of whatever she is. Whatever we are.

I realize I am too late. That I was the shadow. I was the life unlived.

She.

She.

I think she must hate me. I'm here and she is *"I wish you were here."*

I'm Alive.

But she has stolen all the good and bad parts of my life. She has woven them together. She carries all of it. All the things I wanted for my life but am still thankful I missed

She is Florida and wind. She is *service,* and she is right now. She is a woman in a slip, and she is a baby I never knew.

She is two weeks in Florida I don't remember.

She is two weeks of my life.

Over and over.

Wind. Scars. Box.

I should not remember these things.

I was never supposed to.

But I miss them every day.

# What Stage of Grief is It?

1

What stage of grief is it when you dream every night of lost
dogs?

Your dog
Gone three years
at night you search the rooms for him.

He is in the walls.
He is lost in crawl spaces.

He is crunching on dried leaves.

he ate a poisonous mushroom
he lived.

Then he ate another
He lived though that too

But still he died.
Paws
Panic

You dream of your youngest dog

He is alive
But
you dream of forgetting his leash
dropped off at doggy day-care
a place he doesn't go.
it is a place he has never gone—
but still—
The dreams.

For some reason, he was allowed to run free.

You did not bring his leash—
you did not ...

What stage of grief is the dreams of finding his little wet
body in the ocean?
fur salty and frozen.

When you wake in the night
his body is next to yours.
Warm.
Alive

You are not guilty.
You whisper
*snuggle up snuggle bug*

your husband reaches out for you
he thinks your words are meant for him.

2

What stage of grief is it when you dream of tidal waves?
What stage of grief is it when you dream of being lost in a
hotel?
standing at a door
a key unable to fit.

What stage of grief is it when you are back to the dog
dreams?

3

What stage of grief is it when you dream about prying your
father's urn open?
putting his largest bone fragments in your mouth
holding them there
a bitter candy that will never dissolve
teeth breaking under the pressure.

His bones taste like Old Spice
His bones taste like words not said

But they also taste like the ocean
briny and damp
too cold to ever enjoy.

What stage of grief is it when you don't dream?

What stage of grief is it when you are in a grocery store
stifling a scream?
it takes all your strength
To walk down the aisles
Trying not to smash glass bottles
Bud Beer
pickles
jalapeno peppers

What stage of grief is it when you cry
In front of the lobster tank?


4


What stage of grief is it when you take your emergency
Xanax every day?
What stage of grief is it when every day in an emergency?
What stage of grief is it when in the night you wake up—
Screaming?


gardenias

chlorine

your mind spins.

Summer is

bitter

beautiful

a memory


Summer is

Terror

and

First loves

damp jean shorts.


5

What stage of grief is it when you have the same conversation every day?

You need to take your pills
just *these* pills don't take any others—
don't take, don't take, don't take …
you mumble under your breath when you leave her house

*I wish she would just overdose and get it over with.*

Your husband puts his hand on your back
His fingers are love
they get tangled in your fuzzy hood

Summer is far away.

What stage of grief is it when you think vodka is a good
breakfast?

What stage of grief is it when you cry when your vibrator
dies?
more than you do over the fact that your mother—
*Your Mother*
doesn't know if it's day or night

she calls you Sylvia
she calls you Diane

two beautiful *but dead* sisters.

She calls you Mom
Your world spins

And then
It is gone.
Maple syrup and moonshine.
You sip
It's all maple.
It begins again.

6

What stage of grief is it when you wake in the night?

"Fly Me to the Moon"
stuck in your head.

You remember Ross
brain tumor at 36
you remember Mark
heart failure at 53
you remember Bob
suicide at 74
You remember every foxtrot
Happy

Sad

Happy

Sad

They are your dances.

You

You danced with them.

They stepped on your feet.

Yesterday, today, tomorrow.


Toes on toes—

so many little bones.


What if my grief were

Every footstep?

Each broken thing?


Would they taste like cologne?

Old Spice


Each broken bone is my father.

Each broken bone is …

Bad

Beautiful


What Stage of grief is broken bones?


In my head

Toes and bones
So many years of men saying they are sorry
A harmony

It's church.
It's faith.

These are words never meant to be said
These are words
that
should have been sung.

Sometimes words aren't words.
They are a song.
We sing.
Songs are knives.

You remember their arms on your back.
Panicked paws on your angel wings.

Dancing is beautiful until it is screaming.
It's okay to scream.

All the dead ones.
You feel their fingers.

Dancing.

Their hands in yours
you remember that song,
you remember them.

The men you have danced with,

years for each of them

your longest relationships
all dead.

You wonder if they hear foxtrot now
wherever they are.

In the corner of your writing space, there is a mannequin,
her name is Inez.
She watched Bob take his life
now she watches you.

You type—delete—type—delete.

You miss these men. You miss the foxtrot.

"Fly Me to the Moon"

What stage of grief is it when you know—

They don't hear anything where they are.


7


What stage of grief is it when you think your skin smells
like dead mice?
What stage of grief is it when you dream of lost dogs?


when you wake,
and say
*snuggle up snuggle bug*
your dog and your husband don't wake up
They just continue their slow, sweet snores.

# Lithium Moon—1 Day Until the Wolf Moon

Simone fingered the scars on the inside of her left wrist. Though they were not fresh, they were still red, raised, and angry. She read them with her fingers. Left to right, then right to left. Up and down her arm again and again. The story was always the same. It always ended in this strange and ambiguous way.

The scars were barbed wire under pale skin. The scars were a series of crescent shapes in a variety of sizes and depths. There was one full circle there as well, a little further up her arm; that one had been carved deep. They looked like the stages of the moon. When she looked at the pale, tender skin on the inside of her arm, she was proud of the work she had done there, though she never admitted it to anyone.  There was a beauty to the precise nature of all these circles and half circles. She loved to look at them but hated to feel them, even though when she was nervous, like today, she could not help herself. She hated feeling them now. Her right hand read the story of those scars as if they were Braille.

*What is taking the doctor so long to come back?* Simone had an old copy of *People Magazine* in her lap. The cover was asking who was the better royal bride, Meghan or Kate. Did people care about these things? She had wound the magazine until it was tight. It was like a scroll or a rolling pin that she rolled up and down her thighs before straightening it out, then winding it in the opposite direction. Nervous energy. She needed something to do with her hands. She tried to straighten it out, put it back in the plastic magazine holder on the wall. She wasn't the type of person who read *People Magazine*; she hoped the doctor wouldn't think less of her, wouldn't think she would make a *stupid* mom.

The walls of the office were decorated with medical illustrations of pregnancy cycles. The walls leaned against her, making her breath come out of her in jagged bursts. When she looked at the cartoonish drawings and all the brightly colored little lima beans with unformed faces and closed eyes, she got dizzy and, for a moment, thought she would have to put her head between her knees. Claustrophobia—that's all this was.

She looked around the room, her eyes searching for anything that wasn't *The Cycles of Pregnancy.* Her fingers went to the scars again. *No. Don't pick at those.*

She didn't feel like she was alone in here, in this room. Her eyes scanned the corners where the ceiling and walls met. The shadows were darker there, as if the walls met at uneven seams. She wondered if she could put her fingers there; she wondered if she could pry this room apart. Change it. No. No. Of course not. Simone concentrated on her breath. She was tired—that's all this was. But still, she did not feel alone. She searched for security cameras or peepholes. But all there was, besides the illustrations of the baby lima beans, was a narrow window.

There was something not quite right in the way it looked and what it looked out on. At first glance, Simone had thought it was a mirror reflecting back in. But no, there were no baby lima beans in that reflection. It was a window, narrow with beveled glass. Why was it there; what was she supposed to see when she looked out? She always felt a strange uneasiness that tickled the bottoms of her lungs when a window had a view of *nothing.* In this case, it was a brick wall and, six-floors below, a narrow alley void of litter or graffiti like a vacant movie set.

It was already getting dark at just a little past four p.m. She couldn't remember the last time that the sun was out. It seemed like anything after the 1st of November meant that Columbus, Ohio, would be washed in a meaningless blank gray light. This window stared out at blankness blankly. The medical gown that she had balled-up in her lap fell to the floor as she got down from the table. Her feet seemed to not make a sound on the linoleum floor. She expected her boots to echo in the nearly empty room. She thought the sound would ping off the ultrasound machine and the tray of tools that were just used on her. But there was no sound. It was as if she wasn't really here at all . . . Was she?

Her stomach was still cool. The ultrasound jelly had not so much been wiped off as much as it was smeared. She felt it under her breasts; it made her bra feel as if it would slide up her body. She dreaded the pinch of *under-boob*. She would need new bras soon, and pants, and probably shoes. She looked at her Doc Martens and wondered at what point her feet would go from flat to fat. They would swell, and she would lose these; would she be in Crocs by the summer? Would her feet look like nothing more than canned hams stuffed into shoeboxes?

She stared out the window; she counted shadows. There were hands with long, creeping fingers. Five fingers on one hand and six on the other. Or were they just shadows of a tree? Branches and claws. They moved over the brick building across from her, and she felt the shadows on the insides of her arms. Tracing. Tracing. That was when she felt it. The fingers. The claws. She felt it; the hand was reaching for—

She looked around the alley. There was no tree. There was no light to create shadow. She looked back at the brick wall, and there was nothing, just that feeling again under her lungs. A flutter, a nervousness. Her breath coming out in little rapid bursts.

She needed something to do with her hands.

Her doctor opened the door to find her standing there crying. She had not even realized it until she turned around.

"Jesus, sorry . . . Hormones." Simone wiped the tears away and smiled. Her face felt tight, and as her smile stretched across her face, she appeared garish and overly animated like a hand-painted doll. The air in the room felt stale with forced pleasantness and disinfectant, like two different kinds of lemon scents.

Simone was trying her best to appear *normal* and *happy*. Jess should have been there with her. She should have told him about the appointment earlier. Why hadn't she? He would have taken the time off work for this, right? After last time, and the time before . . . He would have wanted to be here—if not for her, at least for their lima bean.

"Things looked good today, so no real worries there. And I looked over the bloodwork; everything was normal." Doctor Martin sat down on his rolling stool and was in an instant closer to her than she thought he should be. It seemed overly personal; though considering he had just had his hands inside of her, she could not understand her sudden uneasiness.

She felt the fluttering again below her ribs, and she could feel the window at her back, leaning against her. She could feel those shadows. Those fingers.

"It's okay for you to call the office and ask to be seen, so I'll never tell you not to, but this is the third time in the past five weeks since you found out you were pregnant that you've asked for an appointment."

"There's a flutter. Under my lungs. It feels like fingers. I know it's not fingers; it's too early. It doesn't even have fingers, just cat claws." She smiled again. It felt like smiling.

"Cat claws?"

"Sorry, it was a joke. I was joking." She coughed a little and tried to startle whatever was fluttering inside of her. "Jess always tells me I'm not very funny. My jokes are weird, or—I don't know. Maybe they're not jokes—"

"You are still seeing your psychiatrist, right?"

She turned around, took another long look over her shoulder towards the window. The branch moved; it slid its invisible hand over the bricks across the alley, its fingers looking for her scars. The claws reaching out to trace the little moons inside her arm. She *knew* there was nothing there. But still, she did feel something.

"Of course, I am." She turned back to her doctor. Had there been too long a pause after Doctor Martin had asked her the question?

"Are you going once a month still?"

"Well, it was weekly for a few months after, after everything that happened last time, and then it was twice a month, and now it's every six weeks."

"So, he knows about the baby?"

"It's she, my psychiatrist. And yeah, yeah, of course she knows." She didn't know. Simone had seen her, but she hadn't mentioned the baby. She hadn't mentioned the cat claws. Her fingers reached up and traced her scars again. She felt them sing. She felt them howl when anyone mentioned or almost mentioned what had happened last time.

"Has she talked about the possibility of reducing your Lithium, or maybe your Risperidone? Or maybe trying something else while you're pregnant?"

"No, no, she didn't mention anything; she said we should wait. I'm doing so well now. She's very proud; everyone is very proud. The meds are really working this time." *Smiling*.

"Of course you are, and I know that after the last miscarriage, you don't want to take any chances, but I do want you to have a discussion with her about other possible options for you, medication-wise. There is a chance with Lithium that the baby could develop Ebstein's Anomaly. I didn't see any signs of that today, but to be on the safe side, I want you to make an appointment with her and see what she can do about getting you on something else."

"Right, yes, of course. Of course. I want everything to work out this time. Of course." She picked at the scar, the full moon on the inside of her arm. She felt its edges catch under her fingernail, these scars not quite six months old. *How stupid does Doctor Martin think I am?* The lithium had stopped a few weeks ago after Simone stayed up all night on WebMD and then went further down the rabbit hole into medical journals and mommy blogs and one tearful, cautionary YouTube documentary filmed on an iPhone with a cracked screen. "I'll make an appointment right away."

"Good, good. That's for the best." They stared at each other. "And how is Jess? He must be excited."

"He's keeping busy." She said nothing about Jess's excitement status. It was not something she felt like she could comment on. Was Jess excited? Or upset? Was he mad at himself for not pulling out that one time they managed to have grief sex since—since what happened before?

"It's always good to keep busy. Give him my best, okay?"

"Sure thing." She smiled again; her cheeks hurt, and her eyes felt small. Simone could not imagine having that conversation with Jess. She didn't know how she would be able to convey *the best* when she could not even understand what was going on with the tree that wasn't there. Surely in the order of important things that she should tell Jess, it would be: (1) The tree branches that she felt against her scars; (2) she had stopped taking her medication, and since then, she felt a fluttering under her ribs; (3) Doctor Martin wanted to send his best.

She would never make it past number one. She was sure of that.

They said their polite goodbyes, and he handed her a paper appointment card, which seemed strange because she didn't ask for another appointment. There was no discussion of what time would be good for *her*. It was for just two weeks out, and the time was written in blue ink.

She would probably have to find another doctor.

Could she really go on seeing a doctor that used blue ink? She hated it. There were words that should not be written in anything but black ink.

Doctor Appointments. Black ink.

Notes that said words like: I'm worried about you; you need help; I can't do this anymore. Black ink.

Bipolar Disorder with Psychotic Features. Black ink. Your rent is late. Your mother called; she said your father is back in the hospital. Black ink, black fucking ink, all of them. Even if the only black ink pen leaked and then ink spilled onto fingers and was left behind on the counter, soaking through a paper towel, and left a stain. The stain was what these words should be written in. They were still black ink.

Messy words like miscarriage.

Doctor Martin left the door open when he left, yet she still stood there; she still picked at the half moon and then the full moon on the inside of her arm. When she brought her hand out to collect her purse, she saw her index and middle fingers had bright red under her nails. She peeked in the cuff of her shirt; she saw the red scar closest to her wrist. It was jagged and bumpy like a frost heave.

Red blood. Red ink for a correction.

Yes, things could be written in black ink and corrected in red. "I can't do this anymore" became "I can't do this anymore." Red ink.

She never should have stopped teaching, but she understood why they asked her to leave. She was like a haunted doll. She spent too much time at her desk; she clicked through slideshows of paintings without speaking; she alternated staring at the screen and at her students with the flickering vacancy of a motel sign. They were afraid the children would be able to smell the sadness and instability that wafted off her like animal musk. They were afraid that the children would catch it—become feral and bray at the moon.

Before she left the exam room, she took one more look at the window. The finger-like branches still played across the bricks; they continued to reach and search for something. She did not want to get too close to the shatterproof glass, the window that would never open no matter how much she might have needed air. Maybe the spindly shadows were not tree branches at all; maybe they *were* claws . . . too big for the baby's cat claws, too big for the baby's fingers that were still webbed together. She looked at the chart of lima beans and tried to figure out when the baby would have real hands. Real fingers. Real claws. She had never gotten that far in the cycle. Maybe this time it would be different.

The sky was darker now, and when she glanced down to the bottom of the alley below, it was already night down there. The sky was still bright, just one day before the full moon. Calendars should be written in black ink and corrected in red.

She felt the fluttering. The nervousness that felt like little fingers, little toes.

The neighbor's dogs started to howl when she pulled into their driveway. The dogs were released into their respective fenced-in yard. They galloped and brayed and smushed their eager goldendoodle noses into the slats of the wooden fence. They snorted like hogs and dug with their paws in frenzied over-excitement. She remembered herself as a child when she ripped open wrapping paper on her birthdays. There was the same kind of abandon, a happiness that screamed out, a delirium that felt like fire. When she opened her mouth when she was a little girl, she howled and tore the paper. She clawed the box that held a pair of sensible leather loafers. Her fingernails had blood underneath them.

Mania.

"Hey there, doodles." She walked closer to the fence.

Their barks sounded like wood being split. She could feel their slobber as it flew; it hit her legs, and it felt like little stones thrown over a pond. Their snouts took up all the empty space between the slats. This fence would need repairing before the baby. It was fine now. The baby still has webbed fingers. The baby was still a lima bean. The fence should be repaired sometime after the baby went from cat claws to real fingers and toes. They needed to do things right this time.

She would tell Jess. She would leave him a note in black ink, and he would do it. "I can do this." Written in black. No corrections in red.

When she walked in the back door, the air smelled stale, as if the heat had been on too high; the kitchen smelled hot and sticky like the corners of burned brownies. The air had a current under it. It felt like the nervousness. There was something here she needed to know, to see . . . The kitchen was narrow, the windows over the sink looked out onto the rabid goldendoodle yard. Everything else was cabinets except for the far wall that was near the coffee maker. This is where their "expression board" was, which was just the fancy couples therapy bullshit word for bulletin board.

"Picked up an extra shift. Won't be home until 2 or 3. Tons of clean up. I won't wake you. There is $60 in the envelope outside your room. Buy some groceries. Don't say I'm not trying."

Blue fucking ink.

# Lithium Moon—5 Full Moons Ago

The second floor to their house was made up of three bedrooms and a small bathroom with a clawfoot tub. There were two bedrooms side-by-side that faced the backyard with its broken fence slats and the neighbor's goldendoodle haven. One room, the nursery, now just held boxes and all the things they had bought when they had gotten ahead of themselves. A still sealed pack and play. Stacked containers that housed unisex baby clothes from all her friends that already had children. There were oceans of yellow, orange, and green onesies. The other room was theirs. Their room only had a view of the goldendoodles and early morning light. Any time after 10:30 in the morning, the room was dark and felt like a barely lit closet. No matter how many lamps were on, it always looked like a memory. It was dreary and faded like an old photo.

The third room was large, with windows on three sides facing North, West, and South. It should have been a master bedroom, but Simone had never understood the concept of wasting the room with the best light in the house for a place in which they would only ever sleep and, on occasion, fuck. It made more sense for it to be her art studio. She loved the heavy door, and these days, she liked that it was the one room in this old house that had a lock—not even the bathrooms had that luxury. This room had privacy.

This was a room that could keep a secret. This was her room.

She looked at her arm. Her moon cycles. Her shallow corrections in red that had been traced over her blue inky veins.

The goldendoodles yipped and skipped next door, which meant Jess was home from work. She couldn't see them, but everyone in the neighborhood could hear them. She looked at the heavy door with the two deadbolt locks. She wondered about the people who lived here before them, about what was going on in this room that it needed to be locked from the inside. *Twice.*

But maybe it wasn't what was going on this room; maybe it was what was going on out there.

*Pick, pick, pick.* She never intended on harming herself. It started with just her fingernails; they scratched against her skin, *cat claws.* But in the month since the last full moon, her fingernails had evolved into straightened out paperclips, the post to her favorite earrings, and once even the dullest of her paint-coated palette knives.

She heard Jess come home from work. The back door opened and then slammed shut without care. She could hear him as he banged around in the kitchen. Her heart hurt when she heard the glass wiggle and warble in the old door frame. She could hear him through the heating vents in the floor. He went to the cookie jar first, as he always did. He typically stuffed at least three Dollar Store sandwich cookies in his mouth at once and then would bring another handful upstairs. He was a creature of habit.

A Creature.

Habit.

She knew he placed the ceramic piggy head of the cookie jar back on cock-eyed. She could hear its crookedness as it wobbled as he left the room. Each step was a stomp; even without shoes, she could hear him. Each step was louder than the one that came before; each heel-toe, heel-toe echoed through the house with an unsaid, "Honey, I'm home."

The glass and the piggy head warbled; they wiggled. Jess bounded up the stairs two at a time. He acted like an eight-year-old. Cookie crumbs fell from his mouth like snow—she always found their trail directly from the crooked head piggy jar to her art studio door.

The door to the studio was closed, which meant she was working, or at least that she had been trying to work before this interruption. He would need to knock. He remembered this, right? She deserved a real knock. Not the one that was a knock *as* he twisted the knob and entered the room. As if, to him, a knock and a "come in" were the same thing. *That* knock had become commonplace in the month since the last full moon. In the two twenty-eight-day cycles since the *incident* on the roof.

Everything outside the door stopped. The warble, the steps. She could feel him outside the door. A floorboard creaked just on the other side of the two unlocked deadbolts. The floor groaned under the weight of his ceaseless impending questions. This loving interrogation would make him seem just caring enough. He knocked, and before his hand was on the knob, she opened the door. She beat him to it.

"Yes?" She didn't say "hello," or "hi," or "hey." She said, "*yes*" like she was a concierge at a gilded hotel.

His energy pressed against her chest. He managed to make her take two steps backwards into the room without her realizing that she had done it. He was there now, in her studio, in her space. She looked down at her paint-covered army pants; they hung low on her hips. Her body was so much different now than it had been just a month ago.

He stared at the blank canvas that was still on her easel. His eyes shifted over to her paint palette; all the colors that were there had long since dried up.  It looked like a poor man's version of a Jackson Pollock painting. His eyes scanned the room. He looked bored. Everything no doubt looked the same to him as it did before he left for work. He was always terrible at understanding subtly.

He could not hear the change in his voice when he spoke to her now, or perhaps she was just hearing him a little better. Perhaps she was more attuned to things. His words sounded the same way a closed-mouth kiss felt when it landed on the no-man's-land part of her face between her temple and forehead.

This room looked the same to him, but it felt different to her.

"Did you work today?" He tried not to stare at the blank canvas, but his eyes kept travelling there as if it were a woman's exposed breasts. She could tell from his expression that all he could see was the blank, the empty, the alone.

"Yeah, I did. It went well. I think I'm really on to something." Simone's eyes did not move to the canvas; she didn't need to see it to know that something new would be created there.

He looked at the canvas again and chewed those cheap fucking Dollar Store cookies. She hoped they tasted like cardboard. She waited for him to say something, but instead, all he did was frown.

He always frowned.

"Sometimes, working is just staring at a blank canvas all day." She wanted to laugh but could not make herself make the noises. "I did prime it, so it's ready now." She picked at the scabs on the inside of her arm. His eyes darted down for a second and then back up to the safety of the blank canvas. He smelled like onions and garlic; he smelled like rich people food and a waitress's perfume.

"It's been months; you need to start to move on."

"No."

"No, what? No, you won't move on?"

"No, it's not been *months*. It's been just two months, two months today."

He frowned again at the blank canvas. He could not see the primer; he couldn't see the readiness. "What are you going to paint?"

Was this what Jess considered *trying?*

Simone didn't want to tell him; she wanted to keep it inside her and let it grow. She wanted to tell him that he smelled like onions. But instead, when she opened her mouth, the truth came out. "It's going to be a werewolf."

He frowned. She felt the nervousness, and the scabs on her arm started to sing and to howl. She saw him wince, and the space he took up in her room became smaller. He sighed and shook his head in exhausted resignation as he left the room, his shoulders slouched and his cookie crumbs leading him away.

Once she heard the shower turn on, she closed the door and turned both deadbolts. She needed to find something sharp. She needed to make her arms howl.

# Lithium Moon—7 Full Moons Ago

J ess worked the night shifts now. He got home any-where between two and four a.m. When she asked about it, why he was so late, he always made excuses. Cleaning. Inspections. A late private party that would not leave the bar. He never told her why underneath the smell of food, there was always a sweeter smell, like baby powder and nectarines.

Being alone and being lonely were different kinds of the same thing; it all depended on her hormones. Did the late nights start when her body changed? Was it when her curvy but thin figure turned into something else? Her hipbones stopped poking out from her skin and instead were like highway barriers that showed a widening of the roadway. Is that when he started to work late? When he started to come home with a faint floral scent on his skin underneath the onions and garlic?

Jess had said it was easier to work the night shift, it paid more money, and she was awake anyway. Simone paced constantly and spent most of her waking hours in the art studio, elbow deep in old paper and blood-colored paint. She expected the sleepless hours without her medication. Doctor Martin had said to expect a period of mania, perhaps delusions. But under her doctor's care, Simone would be able to come out on the other side with a plump, pink-skinned baby in her arms.

Healthy.

Happy.

This was what she wanted. That was what was expected. After all, it was why they bought the house with the extra bedroom, the nursery. They had courted being a family for so long. Those promises, even to themselves, needed to be fulfilled or else they would be failures. Wouldn't they? Wouldn't she? But why, she wondered, was the nursery on the east facing side of the house? Why would the nursery only ever see morning sun and never see the moon? Maybe they had decided on the wrong house, the wrong nursery.

She realized eight weeks into the pregnancy that after years of not remembering the last dream she had or, hell, even the last orgasm, the last time she laughed instead of merely saying, "That's funny," her nights now were filled with sporadic sleep but also vivid dreams. She would wake up in bed alone and covered in a thin sheen of sweat. Her body would be vibrating against the stale air in the room. Between her legs, she would feel her heart beating so fast—and this was *her* heartbeat, not the lima bean's.

She felt almost too alive.

She never would have thought to go off the meds for any reason, really, but this lima bean had made it easier. She wondered what would happen with her dreams now that she was going to be unmedicated for the first time since her teenage years. If the lima bean with its little cat claws was already making her feel unmoored, she wondered what would happen when the anchor of medication was lifted. What would happen to her then?

Simone decided to stop taking her Lithium as well as the Risperidone before she was even asked. They didn't *need* to ask her; she knew, she always *knew*. It was a non-issue for her. But the nervousness inside of her wondered if people would think she was being too rash, too paranoid—

She filled her prescriptions. She brought them home. She lined the bottles up like stoic little soldiers. They never emptied. They just stood there in the medicine cabinet waiting. Jess never noticed, and if her behavior changed, he never mentioned it. He worked late. He wasn't there to see her as she sat at the computer and Googled, Googled, Googled . . .

Ebstein's Anomaly is a rare heart defect in which the tri-cuspid valve—the valve between the upper right chamber and the lower right chamber of the heart—

Medical mumbo jumbo. The words, when read in order, made sense, except she didn't know what they *meant*, and it probably didn't matter.

—Ebstein's Anomaly occurs as a baby develops in the womb. The exact cause is *unknown*. The use of certain drugs (such as lithium or benzodiazepines) during preg-nancy may play a role.

The condition is rare.

Rare.

Lithium.

Leaky valves.

If something were to go wrong, *she* would be the cause. Simone. How was this never mentioned? The fault of it. The *her* of it. They should have warned her, should have said something, should have made sure she knew what was right.

Shhhhhhh . . .

Jess was at work. She tried to sleep in their room, but the bed felt lumpy and cold. The bed held too many years of too few dreams, and now it was the opposite. The mat-tress felt like fists rubbing their knuckles into her lower spine. She ran her hands over the swell of her stomach. She knew the lima bean had claws. She wanted to love it— the bean—but it seemed far away. The fingers, the claws, those should still be weeks away from being real, but still, she felt them. The claws had shown up early. They were already inside of her. She could feel them. Scratching.

There were mornings that she woke up spotting blood. It was *normal*; that was what the experts said. She didn't know how to tell them that she could feel the baby scratching at her from the inside. She didn't know how to tell them that she thought she was dreaming its dreams. Its feral moon dreams. This lima bean, it kept her up at night. She didn't know how she could tell them that she was sure that *it* was larger than it should be at this point, and more . . . aggressive.

They would think she was crazy.

Who could she tell? Jess, he was working. Her mother, they hadn't had a real conversation in years. She would whisper her fears into the pillows, the walls. She would open the window of their bedroom and tell the goldendoodles that there was something growing inside her and she had started to wonder if it was her baby at all. She started to wonder if it was human at all.

The goldendoodles didn't think she was crazy. She thought they understood her.

The walls of their bedroom didn't make sense anymore. She started to peel the wallpaper away in the corner. She wrote in black ink the same word over and over on the back of the paper. She used blue painters' tape to seal the words back into the wall where they belonged. Seal them away where they could not be real.

Werewolf, written in black ink.

*Jess worked nights.*

*Sometimes staring at a blank canvas is working.*

Her hand rubbed her stomach. Her belly felt cool, and the blue veins that ran under her skin felt like a map, each one a scenic route through flat lands and cornfields, babies born too big, too wild. She hated Ohio. She felt homesick for something, for someone she could never be again. The nervousness beat against her insides. The claws stopped scratching her; instead, they took hold. Little hands dug into her and held tight. They got stronger.

She felt a tinge of something, like a cracked rib except deeper—and more broken. It pulled, not towards the highways of blank cornfields but instead up and then out, like a button hook.

Simone never went into her art studio at night. She blamed the light; it was too dark to work. But really, she was afraid. At night, the blank canvases didn't feel like working. At night, the blank canvases felt like holes in her memory. They felt like things she just couldn't remember; they felt like ghosts, and the windows felt like an invitation.

Before Jess worked nights, she was never tempted by the ghosts and invitations, not when they were supposed to be together as a family. Not when Simone was supposed to be at her most *normal*. Not when her pill bottle soldiers were still doing their jobs, before she could feel the moon inside of her, making her little lima bean grow too strong.

She felt the little hands like button hooks start to pull inside of her. She thought if she wrote the word again on the other side of the wallpaper that she would be able to ignore it. But she couldn't—there was a *pull*.

Simone could not see the full moon from this bedroom of theirs, and she wanted to.

The door to her studio could only be locked from the inside. She could lock herself in with the ghosts and invitations, but she could not protect herself from them. Her hands were cold and her fingers stiff when she reached for the knob. She noticed that the room was already open; it had already invited her in.

She could see the moon from here as it made its way across the sky, slow dancing across her windows. The moon invited her.

She felt the pull, the button hook. The claws.

The windows ran from the bottom of the floor to the top of the low hanging eaves in this room. She could see the roof a little above hip level, a small, flat surface that hung over the porch where the porch swing that they never sat on rocked back and forth without them. Why did it move even on a night like this with no wind?

The nervousness grew inside her. It had a pulse; it had dreams; it had nightmares. It had claws and button hooks for hands. It pulled. It howled.

A winter gale screamed inside her head. She was dizzy. Her blank canvases whispered; their words made her skin prickle. She could feel the air through the old windows. It breathed in, held it, and then slowly it let it out.

The calendar said it was spring, but less than a week before, they got twenty inches of snow. That lima bean inside her burned it away; the snow was gone, and all that was left was ice. The claws could tear that away too if this little bean was allowed to get out.

Simone stacked red milkcrates against the wall. They held paper, canvas, and cigar boxes filled with other people's memories. Black ink on masking tape had everything labeled *ephemera*.

The soldiers in her medicine cabinet did nothing to stop her. So many soldiers, heads bowed, heavy with the pills she stopped taking. The pills that she didn't need anymore. She only felt the button hook.

It pulled.

It pulled her. It pulled them. Simone understood that it was not time yet. The lima bean was not ready, but it was still impossible to stop. As she climbed onto the roof, she felt a small stream of blood run down her leg. A correction in red that had already started.

She was on the roof. It hung over the porch, and the porch swing rocked like an empty cradle, an omen that no one heard. The moon looked down on her. It whispered with the ghosts.

She listened to the moon say her name as the button hook pulled, taking pieces from inside of her.

The lima bean's claws held on to parts of her that were deep inside. The lima bean didn't want to leave, but it had to. Its claws grew too sharp and too fast for her body. She could feel how much it wanted to see the moon, this lima bean of hers. She could feel how much it wanted to howl. Her insides pulled and twisted around themselves in different directions until all that was left was a braided rope.

Red ink leaking from a pen. She felt the corrections being finished. She was tied to all of it.

The button hook held on while the claws made their way out. There were pieces of her that seemed to move as they were pulled out. They were the size of her heart. They moved. They lived and died outside of her. The air around her pressed against her skin, and she stared at the shadows that the tree branches made on her neighbor's house; they looked like fingers, claws . . .

She could hear the goldendoodles next door, their happy, hungry tongues lapping against the air. They tasted the button hook; they tasted the lima bean. There was a bitter, coppery taste in Simone's mouth. The air tasted like pennies and red ink. She was the only one who *felt* the button hook. She was the only one who felt the claws. Her heart held the nervousness in its hand. It played in her ribcage, an off-time staccato tango rhythm. She coughed so she could trick her heart back to a regular rhythm. Now it was a foxtrot.

Each time she coughed, a button-hooked handful of her bled out—fists, hearts, stones. Bits of claws shed their outer husk, but their roots were still stuck inside. She coughed and hoped. Simone wanted the claws to leave, but they never did.

They stayed inside her.

They would be waiting there for next time.

She stared at the moon; it was early May, the Flower Moon. When she closed her eyes, Simone pictured that what bled out of her wasn't anything other than orchids and strangled roses.

Jess found her when he got home from work. She was still on the roof outside her studio. She had lost two liters of blood and was close to death. She only whispered one word to him while they waited for 911 to arrive.

"Werewolf."

# Lithium Moon—Wolf Moon—Now

Simone spent the night on a futon mattress she had unrolled from an oversized cardboard box on the floor of her studio. The bedroom that had belonged to Simone and Jess had begun to feel claustrophobic. *This* room made more sense for her. She was able to keep the canvas ghosts company. She was able to keep a watchful eye on the moon as it traveled across the sky—she was able to keep tabs on it from three of her windows. When it rose in the east, it would have been visible for just under an hour most days from the room where they used to be together. The room where they made *the baby*. The one before and the one now.

When she got to the kitchen, it smelled like the outdoors; the window over the sink was open a few inches. Besides the late January air, there was a hint of something else. It was not the hot stickiness of last night, but it was close. There was a hint of fire, and underneath that, something animal, musky . . . not a mouse, something bigger. This smell, it seemed to be coming from her, from inside her.

She felt her stomach flutter, the nervousness, the little lima bean growing arms, fingers, claws. She felt it press against her ribs; she felt the bottom right rib crack like ice. Out of instinct, Simone covered her stomach, protected it from the cold. Her stomach was flat now, flatter somehow than it was before she got pregnant this last time.

As she walked towards the window to close it, she saw it: the glass coffee carafe in the sink, the bottom of it burned to almost black, with a thin layer of caffeine sludge cooked onto the bottom like earth. It was murky like a swamp. There was a ripped-out piece of notebook paper folded on top of it.

She unfolded it and saw written in large block letters, "I see what happened here." The blue ink made her eyes water. When she looked at it again, she saw the corrections she could have made. "I ~~see what~~ happened here."

Yes. That would be better.

"Did you just wake up?"

She made a gasp that caught in her throat. She coughed and felt little claws inside her throat. Her left rib cracked. The lima bean stretched. She had not even heard Jess; had he tried to sneak up on her?

"Jesus, Jess, you scared the hell out of me." Her scars started to make noise—the large full moon carved into her arm let out a low-pitched bray; the smaller crescents sang in a keening wail. She scratched at them to keep them quiet. Her scars needed attention.

"So did you?"

"Did I what?" She could barely hear him over her howling arm.

"Did you just wake up?" His voice was softer now. He whispered at her as if she had a bomb strapped to her chest.

She felt the lima bean press into her right rib again. Little fingers. Little toes.

Her eyes darted to the clock on the stove; it was 11:47 a.m. "No, of course not; I was working. I got up early and answered some emails from the gallery and then, then I . . ." Her voice faded, and her eyes roamed the little galley kitchen. She wanted to look anywhere except at Jess. She saw the cookie jar; its piggy head was still crooked even after all these months of her asking him to be careful, asking him to just—

"You could have burned the house down." He walked past her to the sink. His shoulder bumped against hers as if she was no more than a companion on a crowded train. He reached up and closed the window. "Did you leave the coffee on all day yesterday? I smelled it right when I came home last night, it smelled—"

"Like the corner of brownies." She smiled and realized she was hungry for the first time in days. *When was the last time I ate anything?*

"No, Simone, it smelled like something was on fire."

"I didn't notice it when I got home from the doctor." She waited for him to say something, ask something. *How did the appointment go, Simone? How is the lima bean?* But instead, he turned the faucet on high, his back to her. The imaginary questions lingered in the air and felt cold against her skin. All Jess did was stare into the yard next door, which was void of goldendoodles.

He let the coffee carafe fill as if *this* was the priority. He could have done that last night. But no, he wanted to make a point. He wanted her to see the burned pot; he wanted to leave that fucking note, use that god damn blue ink—that passive aggressive asshole.

"You're not even going to ask me how the appointment went?"

"I'm on the email list; I saw everything, even the ultrasound. Everything looked good. You need to gain a little weight, but the notes said that the weight loss was normal in the first trimester." His eyes softened; she could hear him *trying*. He reached his hand out. On the surface, it seemed like affection. It wasn't. He was trying to swat her hand away from the inside of her arm. He tried to stop her from picking at the moon scars. He tried to stop her from giving them the attention they were howling for.

She stepped back, just out of his reach. The moon scars inside her arm were hers. She thought she heard them laughing.

She had never told Jess about the miscarriage she had when she was nineteen, the *barely there* pregnancy, the four days spent with a *double pink line* test in the side pocket of her vintage Coach leather bag. Four days of not knowing how to say *the words* to anyone. Then, before she knew what size lima bean the baby was, she didn't have to say anything. She was two people, and then she was one. She didn't know if she should mourn or celebrate.

How many full moons ago was that?

So many full moons; two miscarriages, and now this.

"I told you, Simone, you don't need to worry. What happened last time . . . it's not going to happen again."

"Okay—okay. I know."

"The baby is only the size of a lima bean; it doesn't have fingers yet." Jess started to mansplain pregnancy to her. Asshole.

"Without fingers, there are no claws, I know, I know. That's not what I'm feeling. The flutter . . . it's not claws. Not yet . . ."

"I didn't say anything about claws, Simone."

"No, I know you didn't. I was just trying to make sure you understood that I am not saying what happened last time is happening now. I know, I know this time. There's no claws."

*Yet.* She wanted to say yet. But she didn't.

"I don't think you should be doing a werewolf painting." He still hadn't turned back to face her. The burned coffee carafe was the most interesting thing in the room. He fought with the dark caramel stains that reached up the sides of the glass like rot.

"Jess, why would you say that?"

"Because it's not healthy."

"It's a painting. It's fucking art. Since when is art bad? Are you into burning books now? Is that what you do all these nights when you're *working late*?"

The carafe lost his interest. He placed it on the counter. Still mucked up. Still burned. It watched them. When he spoke to her, he eyed the ceramic piggy head, and he probably was thinking of cookies while he said, "I think I should be there for the rest of your appointments, even the next one with your psychiatrist in a few days. I can get the time off from the restaurant; everyone knows the *situation*."

The word *situation* was a hand grenade with the pin pulled.

"What does this have to do with my painting?"

"Everything. It has everything to do with your painting."

"Did you know that tonight's a Wolf Moon? Isn't that weird?"

"I don't care about the moon, Simone."

"No, no, of course you don't. You never want to hear about the *moon*, or my work. I have to hear about your work all the time, all your late nights . . . How was work last night, Jess?"

The canvas was upstairs, blank but primed. It was a whispering ghost. It waited. It didn't want to be a ghost anymore. It wanted more. The blank canvas wanted to be alive.

Simone felt the nervousness. She felt it kick against her right rib that was cracked but not broken. She felt it trying to get out.

In the studio last night, she had laid out the palette knife set. The knives were bright and shiny. They were so new. They could create anything with those ghosts. They were waiting there, next to the paint palette, which was still dry and bumpy with the paint of last year's early trimester angst and morning sickness. Her brushes were clean *enough*.

The canvas waited, and the easel warbled like the glass in the old door if you walked a certain way. Too heavy. There was a box of shredded newspaper that she had been collecting. It was stuffed into milkcrates. Ephemera.

Black, white, and smudgy ink that looked gray. So many pieces of a wolf, but still . . . no wolf.

Not yet.

"You haven't had work at the gallery in over eight months, even before—"

The pin was missing from the grenade, the air in the room was still just a whisker . . . but claws—they grow fast, especially with the moon. "Even before what?" Simone's voice did not question, it challenged.

"Before you got pregnant last time."

*Got.* As if she had done it to herself by accident, like poison oak. She did not wander into pregnancy. It was not a rash that was soothed by scalding water—her skin burned, but nothing was soothed.

She picked. Picked. Picked. "My pregnancy and my art are not the same thing, Jess."

"Then why this? Why a werewolf?"

"You know why."

"I don't, Simone; explain it to me."

"Fuck you. Okay, just fuck you. Some people, they have a place to go, a cemetery, a grave, an urn to hold or run their fingers over before they go to bed. I don't have that." She realized her mistake; she said it and it felt like when she chewed her own hair as a child. "We don't have that."

"But a wolf, a werewolf, it's just . . . Simone, I am worried about—"

"I need to remember it. The baby. The lima bean. It had claws, Jess. I felt them that night. It was too soon for fingers; it was too soon for that—You know that's true. But you, you can't tell me what happened. You weren't there. You were at *work* . . . And I know, I know. This isn't about that, my art's not about that. But—that night—it was just me, and the, the *baby*." She breathed in. She waited for but still dreaded a response, but he gave her nothing.

"I felt *its* claws; I felt it. One of its hands held on inside of me, it held on like a button hook, and the other hand crawled its way out. It took part of me with it, but now it's back, and I don't know, I don't know, I don't know, if the baby put everything back. You can't tell me what I know happened. It wasn't your body; it was mine. And now, I don't know . . . we can't know anything, it's too soon. The Wolf Moon is tonight, but we should be fine, the baby's just a lima bean—"

His face was beautiful when he spoke, like when they first met. His eyes were like knots in an old tree where people had their first kiss. "We need to call someone; we need to call your docto—"

She didn't know how easy it would feel to just shut him up.

The sludge from the coffee carafe spilled down his face in dark, caramel, soapy bubbles. Red corrections trickled into the warm brown. It tinted the soapy water, and he looked like stained glass.

Like a saint in a church.

The glass shattered. All she had in her hand was a handle. It was slippery but still somehow sturdy in her hand. Jess looked up at her; there was no emotion other than a glimpse of something questioned but never asked. He fell to the floor; the weight of him felt like a garbage bag of bloody rags.

"I'm sorry. I'm sorry. I just need to remember it, that night." She felt the flutter again, the nervousness. The second rib on her right side cracked.

The plastic handle was sturdy when it hit him again and again in the soft tender spot near his temple.

She thought about killing him, but she didn't. Did she?

The scars inside her arm howled. She looked again at the clock over the stove. It was 11:48, but this time it was p.m. The windows were dark. She looked down to see Jess, but the floor was just shattered glass and red ink. The handle of the coffee carafe was edged like baby teeth plucked from the gums. She was alone.

The door to the basement was open a few inches, so she pulled it closed without looking down the steep stairs. The wobbly ceramic piggy head of the cookie jar was placed perfectly. Cookies had spilled over the counter somehow. She picked one up and put it in her mouth. It had already turned into a memory—yesterday's cookie.

She grabbed a black pen and wrote on a yellow post-it—Do Not Disturb—and stuck it to the basement door.

Black ink.

Simone's scars started to hum; they wanted to scream. The air didn't smell like coffee or burned brownies. The air smelled like a scream and felt like winter thunder.

The goldendoodles were in the yard next door. They played in the ice, their paws snapping it with each jump, each paw pounded into the ground. The air howled. The room howled.

Simone, the scars, and the lima bean sang.

They howled.

It was two minutes until tomorrow, two minutes until the Wolf Moon.

The nervousness in her stomach and under her heart had finally stopped. Her ribs were broken; bones skimmed against her skin like claws.

Yes.

Claws.

They were back.

Simone knew what she could paint on the canvas.

She walked through the silent house and past the Christmas tree that should have been taken down a month ago. She hadn't thought of it or even remembered it was there, not until now. The red lights blinked on and off like her red-penned corrections. She thought of Jess in the basement; yes, things had started to correct themselves. Her studio seemed quiet now. The lima bean took a deep breath.

It waited.

She stared at her blank canvas, and she saw a wolf.

Her wolf.

It was just waiting to be born.

## Jennifer Anne Gordon

Beautiful, Frightening, and Silent
From Daylight to Madness (The Hotel book 1)
When the Sleeping Dead Still Talk (The Hotel book 2)
Pretty/Ugly

# About the Author

Jennifer Anne Gordon is an award-winning author and popular host of the Vox Vomitus podcast. Her novel *Beautiful, Frightening and Silent* won the Kindle Award for Best Horror/Suspense for 2020, Best Horror 2020 from Authors on the Air, and was a finalist for American Book Fest's Best Book Award- Horror, 2020. It also received the Platinum 5 Star Review from Reader's Choice as well as the Gold Seal from Book View. Her latest novel *Pretty/Ugly* won the Helicon Award for Best Horror for 2022, the Kindle Award for Best Novel of the Year (Reader's Choice), as well as the Gold Medal from Literary Titan. Jennifer is a member of Mystery Writers of America, the Horror Writers Association (where she served on the jury for the Stoker Awards) and is the Agents and Editors chair of the New England Crime Bake Committee.

Her upcoming collection *The Japanese Box: Tales of Grief and Horror* will be published in late 2023 (Last Waltz Publishing) she is also a featured essayist in *Let Grief Speak* by Diane Zinna (Columbia University Press 2024).

Her personal essays on grief, trauma, and horror have been published at The Horror Tree, Ladies of Horror Fiction, The Nerd Daily, and Reader's Entertainment Magazine.

For more information you can visit her website at www.JenniferAnneGordon.com

She is represented by Paula Munier at Talcott Notch Literary.

# Acknowledgements

For such a small book, there are still a lot of people to thank. I need to start first with the Grief Writing Community that the fantastic Diane Zinna has created. If it were not for her, and all the griefies…The Japanese Box would still be a dusty relic in a box never unpacked. Thank you for watching me unpack it. Thank you for watching me turn it into a horror story□—and thank you for knowing which parts are the truth.

Thank you to instagram's @motherwortandrose who gave the writing prompt that inspired my "What Stage of Grief" poem was.

Thank you to the staff of a random Panera Bread in the Midwest…this is where Simulacrum was born…Once again I thought I was writing a Rom-Com, and once again…I was not.

Thank you to the people I cried to.

Thank you to my mazing team that always has my back. Paula Munier, my literary agent, and everyone at Talcott Notch. Thank you to my publicist Mickey Mikkelson and Creative Edge. Thank you to the team at Books and Moods.

Thank you to my book wife/sister Allison Martine (A.M Hubbard) thanks for buddy reading with me and co-hosting our show. Thank you for being there at the beginning, now, and always. Without our chats I am not sure who I would be.

Diane Zinna. Mentor, friend, collaborator. Thank you for cheering me on when I'm writing from the scar and holding me when I write from the wound.

Josh Malerman...dude. you read Japanese Box and got it, and you got me. Thank you for being a weirdo. Thank you for taking time to talk to me, thank you for talking about Bridgeton in the middle of the night with me. Thank you for understanding quiet horror, and the terror of letting yourself cry.

Tara BFF, lifelong pen pal and soulmate. Memes for life!

Roman...you are the best person I could spend my life with. Thank you for following me around when I pace, even though I hate that. Thank you for always saying whatever I am writing is the best work I have ever done—even when it's a mess.

Thank you to the *Hot Mess Express* and all my dance students...sorry I talk about horror and writing so much, I know you are with me for the Foxtrot...I should focus.

Everyone at Last Waltz Publishing. You have taken a chance on this weird collection of grief horror. I love you for it.

And to my dog Lord Tubby. Thank you for distracting me when you know I need it the most.

To the Horror Writing Community and the Crime Writing Community—thanks for being so weird.

*Last Waltz Publishing*

Visit our website for a list of titles and authors